A DESIGNED AFFAIR

CHERYL BARTON

www.bartonpublishingLLC.com

Published by:
Barton Publishing, LLC

This book is a work of fiction. Any references or similarities to actual events, real people, living or dead, or to real places, are intended to give the novel a sense of reality. Any similarities in names, characters, places and incidents is entirely coincidental.

Barton Publishing, LLC
P.O. Box 962
Reisterstown, Maryland 21136
www.bartonpublishingLLC.com

Ordering Information:
Quantity sales. Special discounts are available on quantity purchases by corporations, associations, and others. For details, contact the publisher at the address above.
Orders by U.S. trade bookstores and wholesalers. Please contact
Publisher@bartonpublishingLLC.com

DEDICATION

This book is dedicated to the memory of my brother, John Barton, III (December 26, 1962 – February 24, 2010), my inspiration to live each day like it's my last. I miss you and I think about you every day. I know you are smiling because I'm pressing forward and making more dreams become a reality.

To My Readers:

Thank you for joining me on a journey to bring you romance that's fun and sexy. Welcome to the story of Loren and Mike. You may remember them in *BACHELOR NOT FOR SALE*, my first published novel. There was a hint of an attraction and now we see where that hint leads.

I hope you enjoy venturing into the life and love of Loren and Mike as they take the blinders off and seek out the kind of love that most people only dream of.

Find out more about this and other novels by visiting my web site at www.cherylbarton.net.

Prologue

"Hey, Mike, how are you? Duron said you wanted to talk to me about some interior design work for a house?"

There was silence on the other end of the phone as Loren waited for him to reply in that deep voice she loved hearing. There was something about hearing his voice that had her thinking of hot, sweaty nights between the sheets enjoying all of the wonderful things she knew the lips that produced his sexy voice could do to her.

"Yes I do."

Loren noticed a slight pause and just when she thought his voice couldn't get deeper and sexier, he spoke, again, sending every fiber of her being into a sexually charged haze.

"I've been waiting for you Loren."

His deep, baritone voice had her legs shaking. She wiped her forehead as a thin sheen of sweat began to form on her brow at the double entendre she was reading behind his response. She tried with all of her might to shake off the fantasy forming in her head, but couldn't. Her mind was picturing his long lean and muscular body, stretched out on his bed, looking up at her with a look of invite to join him.

His eyes were a deep, penetrating, rich, dark chocolate that were damn near hypnotic. His smile showed off perfectly aligned, white teeth encased by lips that held promises of hours on hours of pure delight.

Loren could almost see the thick, black, neatly trimmed mustache on his more than handsome face. She trembled at the thought of being his afternoon enjoyment and the pleasure she would endure as his mustache left marks all over her body, especially her most intimate parts.

She couldn't help but imagine holding on to his muscular arms, achieved by many hours in the gym lifting weights, gripping them tightly as he whispered close to her ear all of the naughty things he'd like to do to her that she could hardly wait for.

Though she loved seeing him in casual attire, especially jeans that gripped his perfectly shaped behind, that led down to strong, Herculean built thighs, today, in the fantasy she was currently experiencing, his legs were uncovered, along with the rest of his body and she could see the valley at the top of his thighs that led to what was making her heart beat increase. She'd caught herself in the past, more times than she would like to admit, glancing at his clearly defined package through perfect fitting jeans and knew that what his zipper hid was massive. Her imagination of the power behind his strokes, using those same thighs during love making, had her rubbing her thighs together to ease just a little of the pressure that was beginning to build up.

Loren closed her eyes and could smell him. He always

smelled so deliciously intoxicating. The cologne he wore, Dark Obsession by Calvin Klein, was perfect for him. The powerful, fiery scent matched his powerful, fiery, sexy personality. He was definitely the most handsome man she'd ever seen. It wasn't just that his face was gorgeous, but seeing him, he embodied the total package for her. Being around Mike was like having her very, own Idris Elba to look at all the time. They could almost pass for twins.

Loren was jolted from her fantasy by Mike, making her remember she was still on the phone with him.

"Loren? Are you still with me?"

Loren thought to herself, *'am I ever!'* She was now on a high and didn't want to come down.

"Have you?" she replied.

"Have I what, Loren?"

Loren thought, if he didn't stop saying her name so seductively, she was going to burst into flames right on the spot.

"Have you been waiting for me as you said?" she asked.

She held her breath waiting for his answer.

"Yes I have," she heard him say in a way that had her feeling like he was the piper playing his flute drawing her in with every mention of her name.

Loren's brief fantasy had her speaking her mind before her head had a chance to pull her words back.

"I've been waiting for you too, Mike."

Stunned at her own admission and the sweet sexy way in which she'd just made her declaration, she could only hope that he either didn't hear her or took the gentlemanly route and acted as if he hadn't.

When he didn't immediately reply, she knew he'd heard

her.   She could hear his breathing get deeper and his breath intake on the other end of the phone let her know that she was in trouble; the best kind of trouble hopefully. She knew that neither of them were talking about house decorating now. At least that's what her mind was saying.

"Loren?"

She started nipping on her bottom lip lightly, a terrible habit she had whenever she felt nervous. She should have visited the drawer where her toy supply was kept before calling him.   She knew beforehand that before they finished speaking, she would need some kind of relief that only an item in her secret drawer could provide until the day she became bold enough and replaced the toy with Mike's package.   She fanned herself knowing that the way she was reacting to him was the result of not being intimate with anyone for a very long time.   In the back of her mind, perhaps she'd been waiting for Mike.   Her attraction her brother's best friend was getting out of control and Loren didn't know how much more she could take.

She tried to clear her throat and her mind before responding again.

"Yes, Mike?"

"Meet me and let's talk about it."

Before she could think of whether he was talking about house decorating or something else, she answered, "I'm ready when you are."

Chapter 1

Loren smiled as she looked at the numbers showing a noticeable increase in the profits for her interior design firm, *LKnight Designs*. Business was booming and it was days and numbers like today that made her appreciate her decision to go into the design business. She had several clients lined up and even more phone calls and emails to return from potential clients.

She was glad that she'd scheduled several interviews later in the week to hire a few new assistants because she was going to need the help. Word about her business was spreading like wild flowers and she was happy for the added boost. She'd wanted to be an interior designer for as long as she could remember and looking around at all that she'd achieved, it was worth having the dream.

As a child, when she played with her Barbie dream house and all of its accessories, she would enjoy decorating the rooms by cutting up clothes to make curtains for her doll house windows and making her very own blankets for her doll's beds with washcloths. Even now she smiled remembering the day her father walked into her bedroom with a bag of brand new wash cloths from the store and told her to stop cutting up all of the washcloths in the house. No one had any left to wash with. After that day, ever so often, she would come home to a mysterious bag left on her bed with tons of colored swatches for her to cut up and design new things with without destroying anymore household washcloths. She had been in heaven.

As a teenager, she picked up the latest copy of *Better Homes & Gardens* magazine while all of her friends were looking at the latest clothing fashion magazines or gossip rags. Her mind was always on how she could bring new life to a room with her added touch. She loved shopping trips with her mother and not just to buy the latest fashions, but to also check out the newest fabrics for chair coverings and window treatments. Her entire family would get in on her desire to create and refurbish by bringing home used furniture for her to bring to life her design ideas. She loved that her mother still kept several of her creations in her home.

Loren knew at a young age that she had a great eye for beautiful art and could see a few pieces and imagine how she would place them in a room in just the right space leaving people in awe. Her friends who thought that she was crazy going into the interior design field just didn't understand. They often told her she would never make a lot of money just by decorating rooms with new curtains or chairs. She knew they didn't understand her passion and she didn't care. Her love for it drove her day after day and now that she was riding high as a very well sought after designer, she knew that interior designing was exactly what she was meant to do.

She was about to check a few more numbers from the week's client payments she'd received when her next appointment arrived. Mr. & Mrs. Madison were friends of one of her best clients and they were looking to her for assistance in redesigning the interior of two hotels they had recently acquired. One was on the island of Barbados while the other was in Miami, Florida. Both were locations Loren loved to visit. As an interior designer, it was part of her job to stay on top of what the latest and most popular spots around the world were upgrading to when it came to the designs they used to attract customers. The Madison's had acquired both hotels in a will and were looking forward to bringing new life to them to attract new vacationers.

Loren stood and came around from behind the Italian wooden desk in her office as they entered her shop. She quickly checked her appearance in the floor to ceiling mirror to be sure nothing was out of place. She prided herself on the professional appearance she represented each day.

Today she was wearing her favorite canary yellow Moi-Meme two piece suit by designer Dawn Verbrigghe, with the skirt coming just above her knees. Loren had always been a fan. Her suits were all tailor made and always fit her like a second skin. She added a pair of yellow and black five inch heels by Steve Madden and her outfit was ready for business. As usual not a hair was out of place and her jewelry sparkled around her neck and on her wrists. Her perfectly manicured nails were a staple for her since she not only believed in having beauty all around her, but she loved that it was a part of her as well. Though she was not a clothing designer, anyone in the design business should look impeccable at all times and she never missed an opportunity to shine.

After finding her appearance acceptable, she headed out onto the main floor to greet her guests. She had recently moved to the new location and loved the layout. Her office was all glass enclosed which gave her a great view of the main lobby and the entrance whenever anyone entered.

She greeted her clients herself today since the part time receptionist, Sherry, she'd hired was also a full-time student at her alma mater, Spellman, and she had classes most of the morning. Loren loved being able to pay it forward by being a mentor to other students who were interested in careers as designers.

The Madison's spotted Loren heading toward them and jubilantly greeted her as they shook hands.

"Mr. and Mrs. Madison, it's so nice to see you again..

"Loren, it's good to see you again as well. I'm sorry we're a bit late. The traffic here in Atlanta is awful," Mrs. Madison said.

Loren agreed, having lived in the area all of her life, she knew it was a staple in the area for the traffic to be a nightmare.

She then turned to greet Mr. Madison as well.

"Welcome again, Mr. Madison. Glad to have you both back again."

"Thank you very much Loren," he responded following a handshake.

"Let's have a seat while we go over the ideas I have so far for the hotels."

Loren showed them to one of the three seating areas specifically designed for comfort where she could discuss ideas with clients. She could have used her office to do it, but she liked the relaxed feeling of the casual chairs, occasional tables and the open atmosphere of the open space. She wanted people to feel as if they were at home and relaxed when they came to her to discuss business.

"Before I sit, can I get you both anything to drink?"

"Would you happen to have any of that white wine you served the last time we were here?" Mrs. Madison asked.

"I sure do. I'll get you a glass."

She then turned to the husband.

"Would you like anything?"

"Just some coffee if you have it, thank you."

"Sure. I'll be right back. In the interim, why don't you both take a look at the folders laying before you on the table? I visited both locations and had lots of photos taken of the way the hotels look right now. You'll see those on the left side and on the right side you'll see some ideas I have for making upgrades. I think you'll be pleased."

Both nodded and proceeded to take a look as Loren went to her lounge area to get their drinks. She was proud of the work she had done to fulfill their wish list of what they would like to see changed at each hotel. She agreed with them that both needed some serious upgrades and amenities in order to continue competing with other hotels and to also continue to attract a steady stream of guests.

When she returned, she could tell by the look on Mrs. Madison's face that they were pleased by what they were looking at.

"Loren, these ideas you have are great. My husband and I were saying that we love the bright new lobby furniture and the cabanas around the pool are fantastic. We especially like the redesign of the rooms on the top three floors of the Miami location. We like how these are being redesigned around the idea of women who like to do ladies nights out or ladies get-a-ways and want all of the women to be able to stay comfortably in one suite. The new layouts, fabrics for the furniture and colors that brighten up all of the rooms are sure to be a hit."

Loren had no doubt they would like her suggestions.

"I'm glad. I understand the previous owners were up in age and didn't really care for color. Big, bright, bold colors seem to be the trend right now. Here are your drinks. Why don't we start from the beginning and let me walk you through each room and everything that I think you were looking for as far as improvements."

Loren took her seat, happy that she was about to have another satisfied customer and another major project under her belt. She had her head down looking again over the upgrades in the plan and didn't notice that the Madison's attention had been drawn elsewhere. When she began to speak and neither answered, she looked up to see if there was a problem.

"Is something wrong she asked noticing both had turned toward the front door. She looked beyond them to see what had taken their attention away. Her heart leaped in her chest when she saw the sexy sight of Michael Bailey, her brother's best friend standing in the doorway.

"No, nothing's wrong dear. There is a handsome man standing in your doorway looking like he stepped out of a men's best dressed magazine and he's looking at you like he's imagining you naked," Mrs. Madison said.

Loren blushed not at her words, but at the ideas running through her own mind at seeing Mike in her place of business. She knew they had planned to meet to talk about a project, but she thought they'd made plans to meet later in the week. She was surprised to see him. She excused herself to see what brought him to her store unexpectedly.

"Mike, what are you doing here? Did we have a meeting about your house I forgot about?"

Mike didn't know what to say. His tongue felt like lead in his mouth. Loren was beautiful and she seemed to get even more beautiful every time he saw her. In the back of his mind he heard a voice telling him to back off, but when he found himself coming from a business meeting and not far from her office, he couldn't resist stopping by. Now that he was here, he didn't know what to say. He gathered his thoughts and realized he needed to say something.

"No, not at all. I had a meeting a few blocks down and I thought since I was close by, I would stop in to say hello, but I see you're with a client so I'll see you later this week for our meeting. Are we still on?" he asked.

Loren knew nothing would keep her from it.

"Yes we are."

"Well I'll let you get back to our client."

Mike turned to leave, but before he went through the door, he turned back to Loren who hadn't yet turned to head back to her guests.

"Loren?" he said drawing her attention back to him.

"Yes?" she answered.

"You look beautiful as usual."

Loren's heart was beating so fast she wondered if anyone could hear it. It had to be making some sort of sound, she thought.

"Thank you," she said capturing his eyes and noticed something different, something she'd never paid attention to before. To her it looked a lot like lust, but that couldn't be it. She'd always had a soft spot when it came to Mike, but she never got the feeling that he openly felt the same way. Could she be wrong? She watched as he finally turned to leave and when he was no longer within her eye sight she headed back to her guests. On the walk back to them, she couldn't help but marvel at how sexy Mike looked in his tailor made suit that looked as if it was made to fit his body perfectly. She always thought other than seeing a man naked, there was nothing sexier than seeing a man in a suit made just for him.

"Is that your boyfriend or husband?" Mrs. Madison asked.

Loren was jolted out of her thoughts of Mike.

"No, not at all. He's my brother's best friend and business partner. He was in the area at a meeting and just stopped in to say hello, nothing more."

She watched at the couple smiled.

"I would say there was definitely something more and not just in how you became all flustered when he showed up. Clearly he's interested in you. It's a good thing we were here or by now you'd be spread out over that desk in your office with him all over you. I know the signs because it's the same look my husband gives me every time he sees me. Trust me, I know what I know. That man wants you. The question is, what are you going to do about it."

Loren didn't know how to answer that. She knew what she'd like to do about it, but this was Mike. He was practically family. Could they both have hidden feelings for each other that are finally coming to the surface? Only time would tell, she thought retaking her seat to continue their meeting.

Chapter 2

"Good evening. This is Michael Bailey, Donna Bailey's son. Would she happen to be available?"

"Let me check," replied the receptionist on the other end of the phone.

Mike waited patiently while the receptionist at his mother's office tracked her down. He had been calling his mother's cell phone most of the day and she had not answered or returned his phone call. This was totally out of character for her. He wanted to be sure she was okay. The receptionist entered his thoughts as she returned to the phone.

"Sorry to put you on hold. Yes, she's in. I'll put you right through to her."

"Thank you," Mike replied, relieved that at least he knew his mother was okay. She answered with her normal cheery voice.

"Michael. What a surprise! Is everything okay?"

He tried hart not to sound angry at having to worry unnecessarily about her. He paused to calm his anger before he spoke.

"Mom, I was calling to ask you the same question. Since when do you not return my call or answer your phone when I call? I'm just checking on you since I haven't heard from you in a few days. I was getting worried and if I didn't reach you at the office today, I was going to be on the first plant out of here to find out what was going on. I'm glad you answered."

His voice rose then fell as he tried to tamper down his words filled with worry.

"Michael, honey, I'm fine. I was going to call you when I got to the office today, but as soon as I got here things seemed to get very hectic very fast. The real estate business is booming these days despite the crazy economy. I've been so busy that by the time I get home, I've been going right to bed. I know I usually call you ever two days or so to say hello, but it's just been so crazy around the office. I'm sorry to make you worry, but I'm fine."

Michael began to feel a lot better.

"That's good to hear mom. Do you know that you are still the only person who calls me Michael instead of Mike? It sounds so formal when you say it," he said changing the conversation to something more light than worry.

"I'm your mother Michael. I gave you that name. People can shorten it if they want to, but your name is Michael, not Mike."

Mike laughed out loud at his mother. "I know the story Ma. I'm used to it so it's all good. I wanted to let you know that I'm coming home for a visit. Just for a few days though, because I have a lot going on at work right now."

Mike knew his mother was smiling brightly. She had been complaining to him a lot lately that he never took the time to visit her other than the few holidays a year when he came home.

"Oh that makes me so happy. I'm going to plan a nice dinner party while you're here. Did I tell you Sophie's daughter is single and recently moved to New York? She's beautiful and intelligent and did I mention single? I'm going to invite them over so that you can meet her. I think you would really like her."

Mike just shook his head. He had to smile at his mother's attempts at fixing him up. She had been trying to do it since he graduated from college. She never missed an opportunity to try to fix him up with some daughter or granddaughter of one of her many friends.

"Mom, I'm not coming home to be set up. Contrary to what you may think, I don't have any problems in the women department."

"Well if that were the case, then I would have a daughter-in-law and at least one grandchild by now. I'll never have that if you don't stop serial dating and find one woman to settle down with. You are my only child and I'd like a few grandchildren to spoil before I die."

Mike knew that was coming next. They'd had this very conversation on many occasions.

"Mom, you are not dying anytime soon. There is plenty of time for grandchildren."

"If you say so, Michael. Just no grandchildren without the daughter-in-law though. That never pans out well for the paternal grandmother."

They both laughed.

"No wayward grandchildren mom, I promise. When I meet that perfect woman, I will make sure you are my first phone call. Until then, no match making. I'm not going to keep you. I just wanted to check on you and let you know

I'll be coming home at the end of next week."

"I'm so excited. It seems like forever since I've last seen you."

"Can your son convince you to make him some of your bread pudding while he's home? Oh, and don't let me stop any thoughts you may have of making your famous fried chicken, greens, macaroni and cheese and sweet potatoes, that you like to make when I'm home for a visit. If you must make all of that, I will have no choice, but to oblige you and eat them all."

Donna laughed at her son's sly way of telling her what he wanted her to cook for him when he came home.

"Southern food it is, just for you son. Are you flying or driving in?"

"I'm going to fly in early. Don't worry about picking me up at the airport. I'll grab a cab and meet you back at home when you get off from work. I'm going to go and visit a few friends and make one business stop when I first land."

"Okay. I love you son and you be careful. Let me know if your plans change."

"Love you too mom and I will.

After ending his call, Mike sat back in his office chair and shook his head at the conversation with his mother. He knew despite his telling her not to set him up, she was still going to have her dinner party to introduce him to the daughter of one of her friends.

She's been trying to get him to settle down for a few years, but the player in him could not imagine being with just one woman. He loved women and to him they were like a fresh bag of potato chips. You couldn't have just one. He's not sure he would ever really feel differently. The one woman he really, truly wanted he couldn't have, so he substituted that for the women he sought release with. He never gave them any ideas of forever and he never wanted to lead any of them on, thinking he would make them the one. If he saw a woman getting thoughts of taming him in her head, he backed off. He never set out to hurt anyone and if they could deal with his declaration of only wanting mutual pleasure, then it became a perfect arrangement.

So far, he had only dealt with a few who thought that they could change his mind, but for the most part, he was enjoying his life. Not everyone was meant to be in a monogamous relationship and he couldn't see that for himself. No matter how much his mother wanted that for him, he didn't want it for himself unless he could have the one woman he wanted. He didn't think that was possible. Even now, his thoughts strayed to her. *Loren Knight.*

He couldn't remember a time when he was not attracted to her. He still remembered clearly, the day he realized he wanted Loren.

He and Duron, his best friend and Loren's brother, had gone to visit her at Spellman College where she lived on campus in one of the dorms. He and Duron, at the time, were roommates at Howard University in Washington D.C and when Duron mentioned to him that he was planning to go to Atlanta for the weekend, specifically to visit Loren, Mike couldn't pass up the opportunity to hang on a campus full of beautiful women. It wasn't just the fact that they'd be visiting the campus, but they'd be around women who were around women all day every day, since Spellman was an all girl's institution. The ratio of women to the two of them was too much for him to pass up. He was definitely going along with his friend. There was no doubt that he would find someone or a few someone's to occupy his time while Duron spent time with his sister.

He packed an overnight bag and made sure to add plenty of condoms from the large supply he and Duron kept in their dorm room. He figured he would need them.

He still remembered the visit and the day he realized he had more than a casual interest in Lore. It didn't happen until the end of their visit and Loren had caught him coming out of the room of one of her dorm mates. Seeing the look on her face had him feeling bad about the number of women he had bedded on that campus in one weekend. He felt bad when he saw the pained look of disappointment on her face.

Later that evening, before leaving he and Duron had dinner with Loren before heading back to Washington, D.C., and he and Loren had a moment alone when Duron stepped away. He'd always noticed how beautiful she was, but something about her had changed. She was more mature and no matter how many pretty women he'd encountered on the Spellman campus, there was something about Loren that was drawing him to her. He couldn't help but notice her allure, but she was after all, Duron's sister. He had to turn off the thoughts of how sexy she looked in everything she wore. She had the body of a goddess and he'd have to be blind not to notice. Even when he noticed, he had to remind himself that she was Duron's sister and anything between them could lead to disaster between he and his best friend.

Back then, Loren always wore her hair long and he liked that. She always sported the best designer clothes and the way she coordinated her outfits was a big turn on for him. She always took great pride in how she looked and she made it seem effortless. She was on the slim side except when it came to her backside. She had the type of womanly figure that a pair of apple bottom jeans was made for. She was beautiful and smart and Mike felt that if he were to ever get the chance to prove he could be a one woman man, he wanted to do it with Loren. That thought struck him that weekend and even after returning to his campus, that thought stayed in the back of his mind.

He sat across from her at dinner that night and when Duron stepped away, his defenses were down and for a brief moment, he hoped that she could read in his eyes that he had feelings for her. He couldn't get up the nerve to say the actual words. He needed to tread lightly constantly reminding himself again that Loren was the sister of his best friend.

Duron was a best friend with whom he had shared the story of his weekend activities. He was the best friend who shared the expense of the enormous amount of condoms they purchased monthly. Duron was that friend who shared a code with him when they each had a beauty in their dorm room, so that the other would know to not come in to the room for a while. This was the sister of the best friend who knew that Mike saw women as something to conquer sexually, but not take seriously. Mike knew there was no way Duron would be okay with him developing feelings for Loren, so there was no need to go there.

Over the years, he tried to replace his want for Loren with one woman after another. He wanted her in the worse way, but couldn't have her. He figured, maybe this was karma for all of the women he used for sex without offering them anything more. He wasn't sure, but he wished karma would lighten up and help him find a way to get the one woman he wanted. He didn't just want her intimately. He wanted her lock, stock and barrel. He wanted all of her and he wanted her to have all of him. He just didn't know how to go about it without any issues arising between him and his best friend, Duron.

As he sat behind his desk thinking about her in the past and now in the present, he realized his feelings over the years had never changed. Every time he saw her he was reminded of how much he wanted her to be his, but saw no way to make it happen.

He didn't know what he was thinking stopping by her place of business earlier in the day. He'd been a few blocks away at a meeting and though he had no reason to stop by, he couldn't resist doing so. He knew that he'd known her so long that he didn't really need a reason. Since the day he'd first come home from college with Duron, he'd been considered one of the family and Loren was used to seeing him all the time.

The moment he walked into her office and saw her looking like the most beautiful woman he'd ever seen, he knew he was a goner. He was glad she'd had clients because he didn't know what he would have done if she hadn't. He desire for her was at a new level, one he didn't know how much longer he'd be able to resist. He had to find a way. Too much was at risk if he acted on his feelings.

He brushed the thought off and reached for the folder on his desk that he needed to read over to prepare for his next meeting. For a while, he needed to find a way to take his mind off of Loren and what a gorgeous woman she was. For now, at least, he would distract himself until he saw her later in the week and then he'd be back to where he was when he saw her earlier; completely taken.

Chapter 3

Loren had not spoken to or seen Mike in the few days since he'd shown up at her office simply because he'd been in the area. She was glad he had. She could never tire of seeing his handsome face.

Once her latest clients had agreed to the many changes to both of their hotels, she took a quick flight for a few days to Barbados and Miami to get things underway. She had several small businesses she contracted with that did most of the work of bringing her ideas to life and she'd had them on standby that she was making the trip and would need them onsite to walk through each upgrade.

Her first plan had been to meet with the resort's architect for both hotels who would be handling the major reconstruction work, to be sure the ideas she had were being taken into consideration. She wished that she could have had a chance to work with her brother's firm on this project, but now that they were big shots, this was a small project compared to the multi-million dollar projects they worked on these days. Working with them would give her a chance to be closer to Mike. She knew it was dangerous for her to have such thoughts and feelings about Mike, but the more time passed and the more interaction she had with him, the more thoughts of him stayed on her mind. Working together would be beneficial, but still, very dangerous as well, especially to her heart.

She has already done plenty of work on some of their projects and would soon be working on another one they had coming up. She appreciated the chances she was being afforded being connected to them in the business world.

With their company, Pioneer Architecture & Design, taking the business world by storm, she was being brought along on that train as well and it was paying off for her, giving her the opportunity to build up her clientele through the many connections on the projects.

While preparing to close her office for the day, her thoughts drifted back to Mike and the fact that in a few hours, she would be meeting him for a business dinner to talk about this house of his he wanted her input on. She was more than happy to help him out and even more so because she would get to spend time with him.

Thinking back on how the meeting they were about to have surfaced, Mike approached her brother, Duron about her availability to help him decorate a house he was looking to purchase and totally overhaul. She wasn't sure why he didn't reach out to her directly since she'd known him since her late high school years. He had every phone number to reach her by, he knew where she lived and as far as she knew, he had access to her email and could have done his own contacting. At this point, it didn't matter to her because whatever he needed her to help with, she would make sure she set the time aside, just for him. Mike.

Saying and even thinking about him made her shiver. There was a magnetism that she couldn't seem to pull away from. No matter how hard she tried to get her mind and her body to not venture into the danger zone that was Mike, neither listened to her. She had been fighting a serious attraction to him for years and now her attraction was turning into a hunger that she feared needed to be fed no matter the cost. It was that cost that concerned her the most. She knew, ultimately, that cost could mean the end of a friendship and business partnership between her brother and Mike and she couldn't risk that. No matter how deeply she felt she was beginning to feel for Mike, he was territory she needed to avoid.

She was looking forward to seeing him and hearing all about this house. She had no doubt it was going to be a beautiful house. He had great taste and she knew that first hand because of the magnificent condo he had that she'd helped decorate. The man had great taste in everything, except for women, she smirked to herself.

Loren busied herself around the office trying to turn off thoughts of Mike with other women. She knew his reputation with the ladies and knew he never lacked female companionship. Jealously wasn't something she was often associated with, but in this case, she was jealous of the women who got to feel him in an intimate way. She had a feeling his kisses were electrifying and his lovemaking would surely quench every thirst she had. She'd heard stories about him just as she had about her brother and their other best friend, Tyrone. Mike, from what she heard, never left a woman unsatisfied. Oh, to be one of those women, she thought.

She had agreed to meet him at a super club in

downtown Atlanta. She was glad about the location of the meeting because that gave her extra time to leave the office, go home to change and still get to the restaurant since she didn't live too far away.

Even though her day had been exhausting, it had also been productive. She'd finally interviewed and hired new assistants and soon she'd be able to relax a little more and turn over a lot of the assistant type work that he and her receptionist were currently doing.

Her first hire, Kyle, a recent college graduate came highly recommended and Loren could tell he would be a perfect fit. She also hired another young man, Monroe, who had plans to one day open his own design firm and wanted to learn the business from the bottom up. Loren was more than happy to show him the ropes. She could tell from his resume that he was a hard worker, he didn't mind extensive travel and the moment he walked in and Loren checked out his attire, she could tell he had an eye for flair when it came to coordinating. She was sold. They would both be starting in two weeks. In the meantime, Loren needed to go over dividing up the current projects to have each one of them shadow her in order to get their feet wet. That would have to wait because tonight, she was having dinner with Mike. She smiled catching herself turning business into just dinner.

"This is business," she said out loud to herself. She needed to remember that in order to keep herself in check.

Her thoughts wouldn't be so focused on Mike if she had some type of private life going on for herself. She had done some casual dating, but nothing serious. At first she thought the issue was that she was so focused on work that she didn't have the time to commit to any type of relationship.

Having this quiet time to herself while closing up the office for the evening, she took the time to really assess the issue and not having the time wasn't it at all. No matter how much time work took, there was always time for dating and relationships. She just didn't do it. She would love to have a fulfilling, loving relationship, but the definition of relationships these days certainly was not monogamous. It seemed to her that not only did men no longer value being in a relationship with one woman, but women didn't value it anymore either.

Her last serious relationship ended badly because her ex didn't understand that his penis was not like an ATM machine. He shouldn't give access to every woman who smiled at him looking to make a withdrawal. She would continue to hold to her morals until her prince came along. Until then, no more dating frogs.

Loren thoughts again turned to Mike. He was certainly no frog, but she also couldn't let go of his history with women. He was so good looking that women seemed to instantly drop their panties as soon as he smiled at them; a smile that was as bright and gorgeous as a hundred watt bulb. She had never known him to be involved with just one woman at a time and never anyone seriously. She had deep rooted feelings for him that she knew would never turn into anything special. If she didn't know him so well she didn't think she'd like him at all.

On the surface Mike was a true player, but Loren knew the real Mike. He was kind, considerate, generous and just an all-around good person. He just couldn't keep his zipper up around women and Loren hated that. She hated that in all men. She didn't want to put them down because of their amorous appetites, but she found it hard to find the kind of relationship she really wanted because casual relationships seem to be the norm, just not for her. As much as she loathed his behavior, she still could not suppress the feelings she'd been harboring for him for years. She was looking forward to seeing him, though she wasn't ready to handle the reaction she would have to seeing and being around him again. Tonight was about to be a real test for her and her will.

~~

Loren tried on dress after dress for her dinner meeting with Mike. Her phone rang as she was busy getting herself ready. She noticed it was her best friend, Gizelle calling. She and Gizelle had been roommates in college and had been inseparable ever since then.

"Hey Gizzy," she said, using Gizelle's nickname.

"Loren, girl, hey. So tonight is the night right? Your dinner with Mike?"

Gizelle was the only person Loren told all of her secrets to. She had confided in Gizelle years ago, the out of control feelings she had for Mike. Gizelle was the first person she called when Mike invited her to dinner, well for business of course.

"Yes, it's tonight and I was in the midst of trying to get ready when you called."

"Okay, so what's the outfit for the night? Is it bold and business, or daring and sexy? My vote is for daring and sexy, but that's just me."

Loren shook her head at her friend. If it were left up to Gizelle, she would recommend Loren go in just a thong.

"I'm going with business sexy. How's that?"

Loren could hear Gizelle thinking loudly.

"I guess that'll do. Just make sure you wear some very sexy lingerie underneath just in case you lose your panties tonight."

Loren almost choked from laughing.

"Girl stop. I am not losing any clothing tonight. This is just business."

"Loren, this is me. Remember me? Your best friend in the whole world? This may be business, but you and I both know you want it to be more and just in case he wants that too, make sure you're ready. Oh, and wear your hair up and no bun. You should have let me come over to do your hair and make-up. Having a best friend who owns a beauty salon is a plus for you."

Gizelle owned one of the hottest salons in Atlanta, but Loren didn't want to make too much out of tonight. She didn't want to be disappointed if she went overboard only to discover Mike still saw her as Duron's little sister and nothing more. No, she would keep this as professional as humanly possible.

"Gizzy, my make-up is fine and you just did my hair a few days ago before my last business trip and it's still holding up nicely."

"Alright, I'm going to stop playing mother hen and I'll let you get back to your preparations. I want every single detail though. Call me tomorrow."

Gizelle hung up before Loren could get a response in. Typical Gizelle, Loren thought.

Loren wiped thoughts of Gizelle from her mind and got back to what she was doing.

Getting ready for a meeting about business had never been this frustrating, but this was Mike; her crush. He was the star of many, many fantastic dreams, asleep and awake.

She selected an ensemble that was both sexy and businesslike. She would love to wow Mike, but she didn't want the intent to be one sided so she made sure the sexiness of her outfit was subtle.

She looked at herself in the mirror as she changed into her favorite Steve Madden royal blue and green high heels that went well with her conservative yet mildly sexy royal blue dress.

~~

It was Friday and Mike was preparing to head out of the office early. His thoughts turned to how he would soon be sitting across the table from Loren to discuss business. He was glad had Loren called him back about the house in California he needed her to work on for him.

He had decided to make the move to the west coast to open up and run the new branch of their architecture firm. He, Duron and Tyrone, his two best friends and business partners, had been tossing around the idea for a while and they had finally decided to do it. He didn't mind being the one to move to the west coast since he had a lot of family there and he was ready for something new. He also knew that it would take him away from seeing Loren all the time, but since he'd finally realized he was never going to have her, he had no problem moving. He hoped the move would help him get over his desire for her. To keep the peace with his best friend, who would not be happy with the thoughts that went through his mind daily about Loren, he needed to back off and the move would give him the space he needed.

Mike didn't know what possessed him to call Duron to inquire about Loren working on his house. He knew it was a mistake, especially since he knew he needed to stay away from her, not come up with ways to be around her more often. Forgetting about the repercussions, he threw caution to the wind and went for it. The end result was he was about to sit across the table from his every day crush. He smiled at the word crush. Who would have thought at his age that he still had crushes. His norm was always about the lust and the sex, but with Loren his feelings were much more than that. Lust and sex was definitely on his mind when he thought of her, but he also knew she was so much more than that.

He remembered the brief conversation they'd had when they'd made plans to discuss the house over dinner. He could tell that he'd caught her off guard when he mentioned how he had been waiting for her. It's true he had been waiting for her to call, but the statement had an additional meaning for him. He couldn't help saying it. When he heard her voice on the phone, the reaction his body had to hearing it had gone straight to his groin. He didn't want to come on too strong, but at that moment, he couldn't resist saying what was on his mind, even in the indirect way that he had. At least he was honest. He was waiting for her, not just for her to return his phone call, but he was waiting for *HER*.

Mike got up from his chair and walked around. He needed to get his thoughts in check. This was Loren. He wanted her, yes, but he needed to be careful. His desire for her could blow up in his face. He needed to pull things back a bit before he got to dinner. It was time he got out of the office and changed for his meeting with Loren at his favorite supper club, a spot owned by a very good friend, Jason, whom they all called Jase.

He had just walked out of his office when he spotted

Duron heading towards the elevator at the same time.

"Hey D. You heading out early tonight too huh? Hot date?"

"Yeah I have plans. I told you about Taija, the woman I met through Loren?"

Mike remembered who she was.

"Right, from the bachelor auction?"

Duron knew Mike was trying to be funny. Both of his friends had ribbed him for days about his participation in a bachelor auction, but he didn't care. The amount of money raised would benefit a lot of families and charities in the Atlanta area and he was happy he could help his sister with her sorority's fundraiser.

"Don't start Mike. The business side of the auction is over and I happen to like her, a lot. We're just hanging out tonight. What are you up to?"

Mike didn't want to show any excitement about his evening with Loren.

"Oh, not much. Just planning to grab a bite to eat at Jase's supper club with Loren to talk about the house."

"That's right I forgot you wanted her to work on your house. I'm glad she finally called you back. I know she's been tied up with business. She is on her way up these days. Loren told me about all the new clients she's been taking on. I talked with her earlier and she finally hired some new assistants to help take some of the load off and it's about time because she really needs the extra help."

Mike knew Loren's business had really been picking up since she worked on the interior designs of their office and on each of their current homes.

"Yeah. She's been very busy and tonight was the only free time she had, so I took it. I'm hoping she'll have time to squeeze my little project in, especially since it would mean several trips to the west coast. She said it wasn't a problem so that eases my mind of one less thing to worry about. Now I can just focus on getting the office up and running and I'll turn everything about the house over to her."

The elevator came and they both got in.

"Speaking of the new office, you, Tyrone and I need to talk early next week more about logistics," Duron said. "I know we had tossed the idea around, but now that we're making this happen, I want to talk about the projects we'll do out of that office as opposed to this one. I'd like for all three of us to fly out to do the interviews for the staff of that office since we'll all have to work with them. I also received an inquiry about a new project I want to run by you both. I think it's something Tyrone may want to handle, but we need to jump on it. This one involves some speaking engagements and one is in Texas. I think he should handle that, but we can talk more about it soon."

Mike knew they had a lot of business coming in and that they were each being pulled in many different directions. They needed to do more prioritizing in order to not let anything slip through the cracks.

"That's cool with me."

They reached the garage level and headed to their cars.

"Mike, tell my sister I said hello and I'll talk to her over the weekend."

"I will and good luck with your date."

"Man, you know me. I appreciate the good luck, but I won't need it," Duron said laughing and walking away.

Mike laughed at his inflated ego.

"Jerk," he said to Duron as he walked away.

"Yeah, yeah," Duron replied and made his way to his car.

Chapter 4

Loren was glad that she'd arrived at the restaurant before Mike. She didn't want him to see her walk nervously over to him. She chose their friend Jason's super club to have dinner because it was a place they were both familiar with. She loved the atmosphere and the food was the best in Atlanta.

She had just been seated by the hostess when she looked up to see Mike enter. He was wearing a gray dress shirt opened at the collar and gray tailored slacks that swayed with his long, strong strides. When he reached her his bright smile lit up the room. She couldn't help but smile brightly back. She stood to give him a hug and she relished at how good it felt to hold him tight. She got her quick sniff and was pleased at how good he again smelled. She could get lost in his scent.

"I hope you haven't been waiting long for me?" Mike asked as he took the seat opposite Loren.

"No not at all since I just sat down myself."

"You look lovely Loren."

Her heart flutter. That voice of his was going to be the

end of her. She had to tell herself it was just a simple compliment and that there was nothing more to it.

"Thank you."

She watched as Mike took his seat across from her. The man was simply gorgeous and she could tell from the looks of other ladies around the restaurant who couldn't help but stare at him, that she wasn't the only one who felt that way.

"This place is packed tonight," she said, ignoring the jealous looks of other women. It's a shame, she thought, for them to waste their jealousy on a situation that was all friendship and nothing more.

"I know. This is definitely becoming one of the most popular spots for dinner, music and dancing."

"I don't think I've been here since the night we celebrated the last big contract you, Duron and Tyrone acquired. It's been a while for me. My business has picked up since I did work for you guys. I don't get the chance to get out too often for pleasure at places like this."

Mike was listening as Loren spoke, but he found it hard to concentrate on anything other than the shimmer of the lip gloss that coated her lips; lips that he thought were perfect for kissing. Down boy, he said to himself.

Loren reached for her glass of ice cold water the waitress had just brought for them boy did she need it. Her body was already burning up from the inside out, starting at the intimate spot between her legs and making its way to other hot spots. If she had this reaction to him after only a few minutes, how was she going to survive the rest of the evening.

"I know Duron told you we're opening a west coast office. I'm planning to get that office up and running, so I'll be moving to Los Angeles in a few months to oversee the construction of the office there. It won't be as big as our office here in Atlanta, but it will still rival any other firm in the area. The house should be ready for final inspection soon. I was wondering if you could fit me into your schedule and work on decorating all of the rooms for me. I love what you did with Duron's house and thought you might have some great ideas for mine as well. I need someone who knows me well to do it. I like the color scheme you created in my condo and I want to expand on that, using the same colors throughout."

Loren loved the sound of his voice and she tingled a little when he said the word, need.

"I know it's asking a lot considering it would involve you taking a few trips to California, but I'll cover all of the expenses. I'll email you photos as much as I can so that you won't have to take a lot of trips, but for some of it I'm sure you'll have to see things for yourself. Just send me an invoice for your expenses along with the costs for what you buy and I'll take care of it."

Mike was looking Loren over as he explained everything to her. He was talking business, but his thoughts were far from anything that had to do with the house or the business. He couldn't help but notice how stunning she was tonight. Blue was definitely her color.

"If it's too much, I understand, but I couldn't think of another designer I would trust with knowing what I want."

Loren already knew she'd do anything for Mike. She couldn't wait to put her professional touch on his personal residence.

"Of course I can and I can't wait to see this new house. Duron joked that you were trying to outdo the house he purchased. I swear, you boys have to stop trying to be so competitive and play nicely," she joked.

They both laughed.

"What happened to the house you were building here in Atlanta?"

"Now that we have agreed that I would handle all of the west coast operations, I'm putting that property on the market. I'll keep my condo for when I'm in town, but I don't see a need for a bigger house in the area."

"I can understand that. The last time I talked to my brother, he did mention something about the move, but he didn't say when it would take place or how far along you guys were. Your company is growing very fast and I'm excited for you."

The waitress arrived with their drinks and they placed their orders for dinner. Loren decided to go for her favorite which was the broiled salmon while Mike decided to order his usual porterhouse steak and potato.

"Tell me about this house," Loren said.

"It has three very large bedrooms on the top level with each having an attached bathroom and one additional bathroom is also on that level. The next level down is the main level with the living room, dining room, a huge media room and office and a kitchen that will lead out to the back where I'll have an in-ground pool built."

Loren was impressed.

"Wow. Sounds nice so far," Loren acknowledged.

"I'm happy with it," Mike said. "My favorite level the lowest where there is a movie theater, the room that will house my gym, along with two big open spaces, a full kitchen area, an additional bedroom and two bathrooms. The movie theater was a must. I like the one your brother has in his house and I am a huge movie buff. I often do my best work sitting in front of a movie. My building design creative juices seem to really flow when I'm relaxed with a movie."

"I understand because I love relaxing at the one in Duron's house every chance I get. Well, I can't wait to see this house when it's finished. When do you think I'll be able to get my first look inside?"

He didn't hear anything Loren had just said. He was too busy ogling her. He could tell she was meant to be in the career that she has. Her whole body lit up when she talked about designing. He got excited seeing her excitement.

"Mike? Mike? Are you okay?"

He realized Loren was saying something.

"What? Oh I was just thinking about something. What did you say?"

"I was asking when I would be able to get a look at the finished house so that I can get some photographs of each room to begin my search for the perfect furniture and art for the walls, curtains, etc."

"Not too long actually. I was able to get the house mid-construction. The original builders had to move to China for business purposes and rather than halt the project, they sold it to me. I was able to work out some plans for some of the changes I wanted and it fit right in to the current construction plans. I'll check and get back to you on that."

For the next twenty minutes until their meal arrived Mike gave Loren information on extras he'd like to have in the house.

By the time they'd finished dinner, Loren could almost picture each room and being the architect that he was, Mike was able to get the waitress to grab him a pen and some paper and he sketched out the design of the house which gave her more insight into how the house flowed and the ideas began pouring into her head. She already had ideas in her head for the bedrooms. She remembered getting a catalog recently with a lot of new ideas for bedrooms that were all male.

Silence ensued and Mike had a feeling the evening was about to be over since he'd answered all of her questions and he didn't want that. Since the conversation over the house and the business was done, he moved into a more personal conversation. He knew he shouldn't because he believed in being careful what you asked for because the answer may be more than you bargained for. He went for it anyway.

"So Loren, tell me something. It's Friday night and you're out with me talking business. No hot date or anything for you?"

Mike wasn't sure he wanted to hear her answer. He would be disappointed if she said that she was seeing someone and that she would be meeting him after their business dinner. He was a curious George though.

"Ha, look who's talking about hot dates, Mr. Playboy himself. I'm just as surprised you're coming up for air long enough to have a free weekend night. There isn't some woman waiting for your call for a Friday night quickie?"

Loren knew the moment the words came out of her mouth that she should not have said them. A serious and seductive look came over his face and the look made her briefly hold her breath.

"No Loren, no calls and no quickies. Besides I'm not a quickie kind of guy."

Before Loren could reply, Jase, the owner and friend to them, walked up to the table to say hello. She was glad because she needed a reprieve from thoughts that entered her mind at the mention of the word quickie. She had no doubt Mike was a man who took his time.

"Hey man."

Mike looked up to see Jase reach for a handshake. He stood up to greet his friend.

"Loren, you look lovely and how are you?" he said as he leaned down to give her a hello kiss on the cheek.

"Hey Jase. I'm fine, thank you," she responded.

He then turned his attention back to Mike.

"Man it's been a few weeks," Jase said.

"Yeah, it has. How's business?" Mike asked.

"Business is great. It's good to see you here. I told Tara, the hostess, that you were coming in tonight and to be sure to give you the royal treatment. You know everything's on me tonight so enjoy."

"I appreciate it man. You know you don't have to always comp my meals when I come here. I can afford a meal or two."

They all laughed at Mike's quip. It was well known how successful Mike, Duron and Tyrone's business was.

"What brings you two out here tonight and where is Duron?" Jason asked.

"Loren and I are talking business and Duron had a date. Loren here has agreed to work on the design for a house I'm purchasing in California."

"California? You're moving to California?" Jase asked.

"Yeah. We're expanding the business there. We've been given the opportunity of a lifetime to work on two new projects, one in California and the other in Phoenix. We decided to open an office on the west coast instead of attempting to do all of the work out of the Atlanta office."

"Congratulations on that man. I'm going to let you get back to your evening."

Jason turned to Loren.

"Loren, always good to see you."

"Likewise Jase."

After Jason walked away, Loren turned her attention back to Mike.

"Just in case I haven't said this before, I'm so proud of you guys. You are not letting any grass grow under your feet in the business world," Loren said.

Mike agreed. He and his partners were certainly on their way up in the business world. Landing the most recent multi-million dollar contracts was what they had dreamed about when they were together in college at Howard University.

"Yeah. Things are moving pretty fast. We're just lucky to be able to keep up with the demand for our services. I volunteered to run the west coast office because someone had to do it so that we wouldn't lose out on the potential work from new clients. I love Atlanta, but I have family on the west coast that I don't get to see too often and though I was born and raised in New York, I have always loved visiting the west coast and besides there is great opportunity for the business by expanding, so I'm doing my part. I also know my mother will be happy about the west coast move. Though she lives in New York, she loves the west coast and now she'll have more reasons to visit. Your brother, of course, wants to stay in the Atlanta area to be close to the family which I understand."

Loren understood what it meant to be near family. She loved being close to hers.

"So now that the work discussion is over, would you like

to hang around a while and do some dancing? I know you said you don't get out often, that is, unless you have other plans for the evening."

Mike hoped she'd say yes.

"No, I don't have any plans and dancing sounds great," Loren replied.

Mike stood and made a path for Loren to get to the dance floor.

They danced and Loren admired how Mike moved. He definitely knew his way around the dance floor. When the fast song ended and everyone started clapping and cheering, they went right into a slow song. People on the dance floor started pairing up and Loren and Mike stood looking uncomfortably at each other. It appeared neither knew how to proceed into dancing to a slow tune and the moment seemed awkward.

Mike wanted to dance with Loren and couldn't wait to hold her in his arms, but he didn't want to make her feel uncomfortable at the intimate nature of a slow dance. He had been thinking about it since the moment they hit the dance floor.

Loren started to nervously nibble on her lip as she looked around at all the couples that began to dance around them. Feeling like a spotlight was on them since they were the only two no longer dancing, she started to turn to head back to their table. Before she got too far, Mike grasped her elbow to turn her back around.

"Would you like to dance Loren?" he whispered softly, letting her know she didn't need to feel awkward or uncomfortable around him.

"Sure," she said nervously.

She moved into his embrace as he placed his hands on

her hips, drawing her in closer to him. Other than for a friendly hug, Loren had never been this close to Mike before and her heart sped up at the immediate contact her body had with his. The contact wasn't too intimate in reality, but in her mind, they were as close as two people could get.

As Mike drew her closer, Loren reached her arms up and grasped his arms, feeling the bulging muscles through his shirt. She fell right in step as he swayed to the soft sounds of the band. What she really wanted to do was reach her arms up and wrap them around his neck, but that seemed too personable for the kind of friendly relationship they had.

Mike was enjoying having Loren in his arms. For a moment after he asked Loren to dance to the slow song, he regretted doing so. He knew he should have let her go back to the table, but instead he did what his first thought was instead of listening to his mind which was telling him to back off. His mind was reminding him that this was his best friend's little sister and if anyone was off limits to him, it was definitely Loren. Why he didn't listen to that rational thinking, he didn't know. Now that he was here, on the dance floor, dancing this close to Loren, he couldn't turn back. She felt so good in his arms. He was getting lost in the feel of having her in his arms. This was not good, he thought to himself again, because this was the sister of his best friend. In his mind he sounded like a broken record, but he needed to keep the reminder fresh.

Duron was a best friend who knew how often and how many woman he was currently connected to sexually. He was that one person who would prefer that Mike were like a protective brother figure for Loren and not a bed companion. Duron was that best friend who Mike was sure would kill him if he knew the thoughts that Mike was having at this very moment Loren and this not good. His mind was screaming for him to stop and head back to the table, but his body was doing a happy dance, finally having her close even if it was just for a dance.

Loren noticed Mike looking down at her as they danced and she could tell something was different in the way he was looking at her. She had never really paid attention in the past at how he looked at her because they had always been in settings where other family members or friends were around. It had never been just the two of them and they had never been in such an intimate setting as they were now.

The lights in the restaurant were dim, the music was soft and mellow, the atmosphere was one filled with love and seduction and Loren found herself falling victim to her surroundings.

She looked down away from his stare and thought she fought doing so, she looked back up into his handsome face and straight into his piercing eyes and the draw to him was real; the attractive couldn't be denied. What scared her more was she knew what her look meant, but now she could see there was more to his look than just simply looking. She wasn't the only one with vivid thoughts of them doing more than just dancing. She could read it all over his face. The thought both frightened and aroused her.

Loren felt like they were in a space where no one else was invited except the two of them and they could freely explore whatever they felt for each other. She was beginning to feel less like a friend to Mike and more like a woman who desired him and whom he desired. There was nothing friendly about the way he was making her feel. She should feel ashamed, but she didn't. What she felt was a need pulling at her to be bold and tell him what was on her mind.

Mike was dying a slow death. He didn't know how much longer he'd be able to stand on the dance floor holding Loren thinking of how sexy her lips look and how he'd like to know how good they tasted. He was imagining his head dropping down lower until he was a mere whisper from her lips. Before she'd have a chance to react, he slide his tongue out and run it along the crease of her closed lips until she gave in and opened for him. When he began to feel like his head was about to move in that direction on its own, he broke the stare and looked over her shoulder to get his mind and body in check. He had to stop and he knew it. No more looking in her eyes because he knew he wouldn't be able to handle it.

Loren saw the look right before Mike turned away from her and stared off around the room. She wasn't sure what was going on between the two of them, but she did know it was not safe territory. Safe or not, he felt good and she felt good being with him. She was starting to relax a lot more and without thinking, she leaned more into him. Without thinking too much about it, she slid her arms up from his arms and placed them at his shoulders. He was so tall, over six feet tall, that Loren couldn't get her arms around his neck, but even this was a very intimate position.

Loren wasn't sure if it was the fact that she had not been intimate with a man in a long while or if it was the remembrance of the many dreams she'd had about him, but with all things combined, her senses were on overdrive.

As soon as she'd placed her arms up and grabbed on to his shoulders, Mike drew her up against his body as they continued to sway together to the music. They danced just like that for the remainder of the song with neither of them making any move toward anything more than just a dance.

When the song ended they drew apart and turned to clap, as others did, for the band. When the band announced they were done for the evening and music would be played for the rest of the night, Loren followed as Mike led them back to their table.

When they sat down across from each other, something in the air had changed. Loren wasn't sure if Mike realized it, but she did. There was suddenly an electricity in the air around them that wasn't there at the beginning of the evening. Loren didn't look away when, without saying a word, they stared at each other as if they had just recognized each other for the first time.

Mike didn't know what he should say next. He knew if he spoke what was on his mind that they would be someplace locked in kisses that would steal both of their breaths away.

It was too much, Loren thought. The look she was getting from Mike was hypnotic. She needed to get out and get home before she reached a point of no turning back. One of them had to do the right thing and it looks like it was up to her.

"Mike, I think I'm going to head out. It's getting late and I have a few ideas I want to put together tonight for your house while they're still fresh. Thanks for thinking of me and I'm excited about the plans I'm thinking of for your space."

Mike didn't say anything. What he wanted to say was he

didn't want the evening to end. He didn't want her to leave. He didn't want this time to be over just yet. He didn't think he would ever have this chance again, to spend this kind of time with Loren, though that's what he wanted to do. He didn't know how to respond to her desire to leave.

"If you're not ready to leave yet Mike, I can get Jase to have one of the guys walk me to my car."

Mike wouldn't have that. He cleared his foggy mind and focused.

"No, I'm heading out too so I'll walk you out. Let me go up to the office and speak to Jase for a minute and I'll be ready to go."

Loren shook her head in acknowledgement and pretended to be preoccupied with something in her purse. She needed the distraction, even after he had walked away.

When Mike got to Jase's office, he was on the phone, but quickly got off as Mike entered.

"Hey man, you heading out?"

"Yeah, it's been a long day, Loren is ready to leave and I need to make sure she gets home okay. I wanted to thank you for the dinner tonight. It was incredible as usual."

"That's cool man. You know when you guys come here I can't charge you," he said.

"Thanks man and I'll be in touch before I move to Cali."

Mike started to leave and Jase stopped him.

"Mike, I did want to mention one other thing to you."

Mike turned back around.

"What's that?"

"You're playing with fire so think again before you strike?"

Mike knew exactly what he was talking about, but he

played it off like he didn't.

"What fire?"

"Mike, man you know what I'm talking about."

Jase looked out of the glass window that overlooked his club and looked right at Loren who was sitting at the table waiting. Mike followed his line of sight.

He continued to play it off like the comment meant nothing.

"I have no idea what you're talking about."

"Mike, really bruh? I have known you for quite a few years. I've seen you come through here with many, many women, but tonight was the first time I've ever seen you take such care with one. Come on man, it's me. I think you have a mighty big issue on your hands and it's one I don't think you are really ready to deal with. All I'm going to say is be careful. You and Duron have been best friends for a lot of years. You need to be very careful when it comes to his sister. You and I both know how he feels about her. Not that you are a bad guy or anything, but that's Duron's sister. You are Duron's friend and he knows you better than I think he knows his own brothers. If you are planning to make some kind of move on her, I suggest you think long and hard about that decision. Duron would kill you and you know it. I know he thinks of you as his third brother, but with the stories I'm sure you two have swapped over the years about women, I doubt if he would be too open to you moving in Loren's direction. I'm just saying be careful."

Mike understood exactly what Jase was saying. Not only could his friendship with Duron be in jeopardy, but his relationship with the entire Knight family could be jeopardized if he decided to act on the thoughts floating around his head about Loren. He definitely wanted her, there was no doubt about that and if Jase could see it from watching them for a couple of hours, others would be able to tell as well. He needed to tame that.

Jase was a good friend and Mike didn't need to lie so he admitted defeat.

"Thanks bruh. I admit I think she's beautiful and I've found myself attracted to her much more than on a friendship basis. I also hear what you're saying about Duron. He's knows all of my secrets and he's the one person I've told all of my stories to about women and there have been a whole lot of them. So I hear you and I'm going to keep my distance. I have to because too much would be at stake."

"I feel for you man. Just know that you are not the only one who has given Loren a second look."

As soon as the words left his mouth, Jase knew it was a mistake. Mike gave him a look that said he needed to rethink his next words.

"Whoa Mike," Jase smiled. "No need to act all aggressive with me. I'm not saying I have a thing for Loren or that I'm even remotely interested. I like my life too much to test Duron's patience because he knows my secrets too man. I'm just saying, a man would have to be dead to not recognize how beautiful Loren is inside and out. Don't do something temporarily stupid that could lead to permanent damage to family and friendships. "

Mike understood his concern and turned away to glance at Loren again through the window of the office.

"I see the wheels turning while you're staring at her right now and I'll say it again, you're playing with fire. Duron would serve your head to you on a platter."

"Don't worry about me, I've got this," Mike answered.

Jase wasn't so sure.

"Are you sure about that? Are you sure about your next move because I don't think you are. Think about this, how many women have you been with in this past month? Better yet, how many in the past two weeks? On top of that, how many have you told Duron about? Now think what you told him about those encounters and ask yourself if you could see yourself telling him you have a think for his baby sister. It's a death sentence. Back off Mike and just walk away."

He didn't even bother answering Jase. His answers to those questions were not pleasant. If memory served him right, he'd had his last sexual encounter with a sex buddy of his over a week ago and he also remembered he told Duron the saucy details. He got one last glance at Loren looking beautiful sitting at the table waiting for him and he turned his attention back to Jase.

"I hear you man. I hear you. I'm heading out to make sure Loren gets home okay. Thanks for the advice and the wake-up all. I'm officially backing off."

He gave Jase a handshake and headed back down to walk Loren to her car.

Loren sat at the table anxious to leave. There was something about her being with Mike tonight that wasn't sitting right with her. Maybe all those sleepless nights of thinking and dreaming about him were coming to the surface because the air between them tonight was unlike any other time they had been around each other.

If she were not mistaken, when they were dancing, Mike had been making circles on her back in a caressing motion, which in her mind was a very intimate move. Maybe he did it without thinking, but it had an effect on her that got her body tingling with want, stronger than she'd ever remembered having before. Being so close to him, her body immediately reacted.

The mixture of his cologne, how close he was holding her and the way he was crooning in her ear, had her thinking about sheets, nakedness, passion and screaming. She had managed to keep her body in check for most of the evening and neither of them made mention of the phone conversation they had that could have meant a few things. She was both hoping that he would and that he wouldn't bring it up. She wanted to clear the air and let him know how attracted she was to him, but she didn't want to be the only one who felt that way.

Loren wasn't sure they could go beyond friendship and keep the friendship intact. When he'd walked away to speak with Jase, she had hoped to get herself in check before he came back. She was doing a good job of it until she looked up and noticed him returning and those warm, fuzzy feelings returned. She needed to get out of the restaurant and away from Mike. Just thinking about him had her close to exploding. She needed release of the worse kind, but now was not the time to walk herself into trouble and then end up with Mike helping her with her release. She watched him return and the closer he got to her, the hotter the temperate in the room seemed to get. Her last thought before he reached her was that she was in trouble.

Mike made his way back over to the table to get Loren.

"Are you ready to go?" he asked.

"Yes I am."

Mike helped Loren stand and placed her hand in the

crook of his arm as they made their way through the crowd to the front entrance.

"Where did you park your car?"

She pointed across the street to the parking garage.

"I'm parked on level three in the garage."

"Good, I'm in there on level one," he said.

Mike escorted Loren across the street and up the elevator to level three to her car.

When they reached her car he said, "Drive me down to my car so that I can follow you home to your condo. I want to be sure you get in okay since it's very late."

Loren nodded. He was a gentleman. Mike may be the biggest man whore she had ever met, but he was also the most respectful man when it came to how he treated a woman and took great care with her safety. When they reached Mike's truck, Loren noticed his hesitation before reaching for the handle to get out.

"Thanks again for a nice evening Mike. I'm not only talking about the business part either. I really enjoyed your company."

Mike turned so that he was completely facing Loren when he replied.

"I enjoyed your company too. I also want to say one more time tonight that you look beautiful."

"Thank you," she said blushing.

After exiting her car, he leaned back in before shutting the door.

"I'm going to follow you to your condo and when you're inside with the door locked, send me a text so I'll know everything is okay."

"Mike you don't have to do that. My condo has paid security and they always make it a point to be sure the women are safely escorted to their doors."

"Just do it for me please?" he asked

"Okay, I will."

Before he shut the door, Loren thanked him again and then he was gone.

True to his word, he followed her to her building and when she was safely locked inside her unit, she sent him a text letting him know she was in. From her living room window on the fifth floor, she could see him drive off. She was finally able to exhale and ask herself, what had happened tonight?

Chapter 5

Loren didn't get much sleep following her evening out with Mike. He had such confidence about himself and Loren knew he would be an assertive and very thorough lover as well. At first she couldn't get to sleep because she had a few websites she wanted to check out for some ideas for his house. She had been up well into the middle of the night doing that and she still couldn't get to sleep as her body would not let her forget about the close contact she had with Mike on the dance floor. Her thoughts had drifted so far off to the night before that she almost missed hearing her phone ringing. Seeing it was Taija, one of her friends, she answered.

"Hey Taija."

"Hey Loren. I hope it's not too early to call you."

"No not at all. I've been up for a while. I was going to give you a call later today anyway to see how you were. Also, so many people have been contacting me since the auction saying that they had a great time and the ladies who won bachelors have been raving about the great dinner dates they've had. We never did get a chance to talk about how yours went with my brother. I've been so busy with work since then that I haven't had a chance to touch base with you."

"That's why I was calling you too. It was incredible and your brother is a great guy. We've been hanging out a little since then and I really like him. I hope you don't mind or find that awkward or anything."

Loren laughed at Taija's comment. Why would she mind?

"Of course not. Do you girl. My brother is a great guy and I'm happy things turned out good. I could tell he was really into you the night of the bachelor auction. Have fun Taija."

"Whew, I'm glad you said that because I wasn't sure if you would be okay with us continuing to see each other or not. I just wanted you to know. Just to mention again, I had a wonderful time with Duron. Well I won't keep you long. Thanks again for helping me with the unpacking and decorating I've already done. The place looks great. I'll give you a call soon."

After they hung up, Loren patted herself on the back. The bachelor auction this year was a major success. Between her sorority work, her charity work, her business and family stuff, Loren's free time was pretty much non-existent. Real personal time was all but non-existent for her. Thinking about personal time had her thinking once again about her last failed relationship. She hated when she couldn't seem to stop revisiting that awful time in her life. She had not had a relationship since her involvement with Sam Wilson.

He had been the love of her life at one time. They had met her junior year in undergraduate school at Spellman and had been together off and on until her graduation from graduate school when they finally parted ways. It was a tough breakup for Loren. Sam had shown her his true colors when she discovered he was seeing other women while in a relationship with her. They weren't just dating, but were in what she thought, was a one on one, serious relationship. He obviously had other ideas of what that meant. Not only did the relationship end horribly, but she then discovered that he'd started seeing a woman she considered a very good friend.

Her brother Duron mentioned, when first met Sam, that there was something about him that he didn't like. Duron never trusted him. He said Sam was too slick and always seemed to be hiding something. They didn't know much about his background and he had no family to speak of; no connection to anyone. That automatically set off warning bells with her brother, but Loren was already in love with the man he showed to her every day. At the time that was enough for her. Now that she was older, more mature and a lot wiser, she expected more and she paid attention more.

For now, she was happy casually dating and taking the time to grow her business. Casual dating for her didn't mean sex, it simply meant having a man to do fun things with and hang out with. She hadn't ventured into anything serious since her relationship with Sam and she wasn't ready to do so yet.

When she decided to go into business for herself, she knew that it would take a high level of commitment on her part and she was dedicated to seeing her business flourish. If she found a man that she could truly be into, she was willing to invest the time into him, but until then, she would settle for work, work and more work to occupy her time. Being so focused on work, it had actually taken her mind off of the fact that she was not intimately involved with anyone, that is until her evening with Mike the night before. He had stirred up desires she had kept under control. Even now, she knew a cold shower was in her near future if she had plans to lessen the effects of the night before when dreams of Mike and what he would look like naked and aroused had her remembering what it felt like being intimate. He made her miss it.

Not being able to stand the heated thoughts any longer that were also turning her body into a furnace, she got up and headed for the shower. As she stripped, she knew that this would be a very, very cold shower.

~~

Mike woke up early Saturday morning with thoughts of Loren on his mind. He had come home the night before and his usual would have been to call a female friend for a nightcap, his word for uncomplicated sex. It's how he often chose to unwind from his week. He didn't do a lot of kicking it with women during the week because lots of time was spent building up the business. When the weekend came, he would call one of his beauties and before he could get the invitation out of his mouth, they would ask him what time should they be ready.

Mike enjoyed having a very active sex life and he loved indulging as much as possible. Even if he wanted to slow things down, he wasn't sure he could after having his libido stroked so often for so long,. He didn't know what it meant to turn it off. Last night, however, was different. Last night was the first Friday in a long time that he didn't pick up his phone to either visit one of his sex buddies or pick one up to join him at his condo. His cell phone had rung a few times from female friends who left messages wanting to know if they would get to see him. He surprised himself when he didn't return the phone messages which were clearly invitations for sex. Instead, he ended up back at his condo alone and thinking about Loren all evening.

Mike let his mind play tricks on him with many wonders of what would have happened if he had kissed Loren in the car, which is what they both wanted. He could tell by the look in her eyes that she wanted him to kiss her and he struggled with that decision. He wanted to badly, but he couldn't get past the fact that Loren was Duron's sister and he didn't feel it would be right to give in to his body's want for Loren when he knew what dangers would lay ahead for him down the road. Instead, he took what he considered the high road and walked away. He tried not to search Loren's face for any disappointment when they spoke before he closed the door. All he knew was that he had done the right thing. At least he thought so at that moment. In the light of day now, he wished he had kissed her. That way the not kissing her would not have haunted him all night. He had been with enough women where he knew the look of a woman who desired him. He desired her as well, but he knew that desire was making them both forget the consequences of proceeding down that path.

For the first time in his life, his past sexual escapades and his reputation with women had come back to bite him in the ass. If he knew nothing else, he knew that Loren knew of his playboy ways when it came to women.

Being Duron's sister, she knew first-hand the plethora of women he was known to have bedded over the years. He was also known for dating several women at one time. He knew that Loren was not the type of woman that he would categorize like that. He wouldn't set her up to be hurt by him because he knew she deserved better than to be one of many women he was seeing. His body wanted her yes, but it was more than that. He had feelings that were growing for her and had been for some time.

On a regular basis he tossed back and forth between the idea of telling her how he felt and staying quiet and the turmoil was wreaking havoc on his life. There were days when he didn't know if he was coming or going when it came to Loren and the more he saw her and thought about her, the stronger his desire for her became. He knew he had to do something soon, but he wasn't sure what that something was. He also knew until he figured it out, he would continue to be plagued by the dilemma every day.

Frustration was not settling in and he knew only one thing could distract him and that was the gym. He got up, grabbed his gear and headed for the door.

~~

A week had gone by since Loren's business dinner with Mike and he was still heavy on her mind. In the midst of that, she was excited that some art she had purchased had finally come in.

Duron had asked her to purchase some wall art for his condo like she did for the house he purchased that she had also decorated. The art she purchased for him had finally come in and she needed to meet the delivery man from the gallery at Duron's condo so that they could get it hung up. She knew that her brother was out at his house in Buckhead so she wouldn't have to worry about disturbing him at the condo while she got the art in its place. This distraction would also allow her some time to get her mind off of Mike. She wasn't trying to fight the connection she was beginning to feel with him. She just didn't want to make a fool of herself fawning all over him when she knew he wasn't the one woman type that she was looking for.

She even questioned herself all week about his interest in her. She second guessed whether he was interested especially after he failed to take advantage of the invitation she was mentally giving him to kiss her the night they'd had dinner, while they sat in her car. She felt the charge in the air and she knew he did as well. She assumed it was possible he still saw her as the little sister of his best friend and not as the woman she had become over the years.

She cleared her mind and focused. The hour was getting late and she had lots to do before heading to the condo to meet the art delivery.

~~

Mike had been at the office for a few hours. It didn't matter how much work he tried to delve into, he could not get his thoughts off of Loren and how sexy she looked the last time he'd seen her.

She had not stopped in at the office to see her brother and other than a few email exchanges back and forth about his house in California, they had no other contact. He wanted to call her, but he fought that want. He didn't know what he would say. They had left things at a point that he would call her when the time came for her to go out to Los Angeles and do a walk-through of his house to take photos of each room. Until then, he really didn't have a reason to just call.

Since it appeared concentration was the furthest thing from his mind, he decided to pack things up and head back up to his condo to get a little remaining work done there before meeting up with some friends later in the evening for drinks and some pool.

After gathering up all the paperwork he would need, he headed to the elevator that would take him up to the penthouse of the office park where he, Tyrone and Duron each had penthouse condos. He loved living at the top of the office park and since traffic in Atlanta could be a beast on most good days, he was glad he didn't have to go far to go home, especially after a late night of working.

While he waited for the elevator, he wondered if Loren had thought about him after the time they had spent over dinner. She had to know that something was happening between the two of them just as he could feel it, but he assumed like him, she had to be thinking of the impact of them getting together on any level. He figured they were both thinking the same thing, that the not knowing, and not acting upon things was best not only for them, but for those closest to them as well.

Mike noticed the elevator was taking longer than usual. Since this elevator only went up to the penthouse level with a special key, it normally came right away, especially on the weekend when he knew Duron was not in the building and Tyrone had gone fishing with friends earlier in the day. A few minutes later the elevator arrived and when the door opened and inside was Loren looking like a goddess, he almost forgot to take his next breath. He was surprised to see her considering he was just thinking about her.

"Hey Loren. What are you doing here?"

"Hey Mike. I'm here for a delivery from an art gallery of some pieces I ordered for Duron's walls. The delivery guy is supposed to meet me here in another hour, but I wanted to come a little early to wait on him. What are you doing on the business floor today? I thought the office was closed?"

Mike entered the elevator and inserted his key into the special lock that would continue to send the elevator to the penthouse level. A key was required every time the express elevator that went to the penthouse was activated and every time it stopped on any floor. The doors would not close and go up without the key. Once the doors were closing again, he turned to face Loren taking in her gorgeous attire. She never disappointed him with how she maintained her pristine look.

Today, on a Saturday, she was dressed in very high heeled green stilettos with jeans and a green and white loose fitting top over a white tank top. Her light make-up was always flawless and the big flashy jewelry she liked to wear was not gaudy, but very fashionable and sexy. Mike's mind and body focused on how sexy she looked, especially in jeans that seemed to hug her body like a glove. They weren't too tight by any means, but fit her just right.

After looking his fill, he finally found the words to respond.

"I came down to get some work done in the office. After having very little success, I decided to head back up to finish before going out later to meet some friends. You look beautiful as always, Loren."

Mike didn't miss the blush he saw cross Loren's face.

"Thanks Mike. You look relaxed."

Checking out his attire in basketball shorts, a t-shirt and tennis shoes, Loren wasn't used to seeing Mike like this. Most of the time when she saw him it was either at the office where he was always dressed in a suit or at some other function where he would again be dressed in either a suit or other dressy attire. Even over the years, she knew that he would often play pickup basketball with her brothers, but she never ran into them until after they had already re-dressed.

"I am relaxed. I've been in all morning chilling and I guess faking playing catch up with work," he laughed.

The elevator reached the top level just as he had finished his statement. They exited as Loren made one last comment before she entered Duron's condo.

"I found some great ideas already for your living room and the bedroom on the lower level for your mother. I haven't actually seen the rooms yet, of course, but I had some ideas based on new catalogs I received that had decorating ideas that I thought you would enjoy. I know you wanted to keep the living room along the lines of what you have in your condo and your mother's room was easy."

Mike tried to pay attention, but he found it hard to focus around her.

"Sounds like you've been busy," he said, not wanting to get caught not paying attention.

"I sure have. I also went to a furniture gallery showing a few months back and I remembered they had new man cave setups I think you'd like. Wait until you see the seating I'm thinking of for your theater room. I think you'll love it. I know you wanted red and black seating in that room and a company I have dealt with in the past just released a new line of theater room seating so you'll be one of the first to get this if you like it."

"Loren, I think you know me better than I know myself when it comes to my taste, so if you say I'll like it, I'm sure I'll love it. I look forward to seeing it."

Neither of them made a move to turn and enter the condos. They stood staring at each other.

"Well if you like, when I'm done here at Duron's, I can

stop over to show you what I have so far. Of course, I don't want to keep you from meeting up with your friends on time, so if you want me to, I can just email you some links of items to check out."

Mike thought about her suggestion. In the back of his mind, he could hear the mechanical voice of the robot from an old television series call Lost in Space, where it would say, "danger Will Robinson, danger." He had seen some old reruns of the old television show and the message was relevant to this current situation. He need not invite Loren into his condo the way she was looking in those jeans and with the way he had been unable to get her off of his mind. He opened his mouth to tell her to go ahead and email him the links, but that's not what came out.

"Sure, stop on over, I'll be here. I'm sure it won't take us long to look at the links. I'll have plenty of time to meet my buddies. That's not until later this evening anyway. Just buzz when you're done. Do you need me to come over when the delivery guy gets here so that you're not by yourself?"

Loren really liked how Mike always looked out for her.

"No I'm good. He's the husband of one my brother's co-workers at the hospital. I'll buzz when I'm done. If I'm taking too long, just go ahead with your plans and I'll just email everything I have so far to you to take a look at. They are, after all, just ideas at the moment. I need to see the inside of the house to get a definitive idea on what will work in your space."

"That's fine. I'll see you in a bit then."

"Okay," Loren replied as she turned, used her key and entered her brother's condo.

At the same time Mike entered his condo and shut the

door.

Loren released the breath she was holding. She had no idea what she was thinking when she mentioned stopping at his condo later. Before the evening they had dined, worked and danced together, it would not have been a big deal to stop in on him if she had run into him in the elevator. Now it seems things have changed between the two of them and Loren didn't know how to get things back to normal. Everything seemed extra intense with Mike. Loren knew she couldn't back out now. The words flew out of her mouth before her mind could catch up to her intention. She had to get herself together and stop the childish behavior, acting like an awestruck teenager and get to the business he was paying her to do. This was, for goodness sake, Mike, someone she had known since she was a braces wearing, tomboy. She could conduct business and tame her wild ideas of hot, passionate and somewhat kinky sex with Mike and remain professional. At least that's what she hoped.

Chapter 6

Mike checked the time again. Loren had called a half hour ago to say she was wrapping up with the guy from the art gallery and the workmen he brought with him to hang all of Duron's art around his condo. Since he'd left her in the hall, he'd showered and changed into jeans and a pullover shirt so that when they were finished looking over all of the information she had gathered so far on ideas for his house, he could head out to meet his friends. He thought when she called she was on her way over then. He was about to call her to be sure everything was okay when his door buzzed. He went to let her in.

"Sorry I'm late," Loren said as she entered his condo and headed for his sitting area to open her laptop.

"No problem. I was just about to call you to be sure you were okay. You called a half hour ago and said you were on your way over and it's only a few steps away."

"I know. As soon as I hung up from you and the guys left, Duron called to see how the art looked and we got to talking."

Mike joined Loren in his sitting area.

"Let's see what you have."

Loren opened up several links to show Mike what she had come up with so far.

He was very impressed with her choices for his mother's room, the living room and his theater room so far. He knew he made the right choice when he decided to ask her to help him out.

"Very nice Loren. I like everything and my mom will be very excited about her room. She won't be with me all the time, but because we have a lot of family on the west coast, I'm thinking she'll come visit me more there than she has here and I want to be sure she's comfortable and that we both have lots of privacy, hence my reason for putting her room on the lower level. Besides there are less steps for her to go up and down than if she were on the top level of the house."

Loren logged off and closed her laptop.

"I'm glad you like my ideas. You make it easy because you aren't hard to work with. I have had some clients that make me want to quit and give back the retainer they paid me to acquire my services. Then I remember that as a business woman, I have to learn to deal with all types of people and not just those who are tolerable."

She reached for her laptop to put it back in her shoulder bag when she noticed Mike staring at her. She tried to look away, but she couldn't. He looked so damned good sitting there relaxed, leaned back in his chair, with both arms across the back. Loren didn't know what to make of the scene, but the silence was killing her.

"I like the additions I see you've made to your condo. Tyrone is the only one I hear who has not made one single upgrade to the original design."

"Thanks. Yeah, Ty hasn't changed or added anything since you decorated when he moved in. He liked it like it was. He's very low maintenance when it comes to his condo. He invests all of his time in cars. If he's not at work, he's working on adding to his car collection or riding around with the motorcycle club he belongs to. To him, a condo is just a place to eat and sleep."

Not knowing what else to say, she thought it best she leave. Besides, she remembered Mike had plans for the evening.

"Well I'm going to go. I don't want to keep you from meeting up with your friends and I'm expecting my niece and nephew tomorrow evening after church so that my brother and his wife can have a date night. I'm stopping at the market tonight to get all of the junk food they like to eat."

Loren stood to leave and Mike took the opportunity to do what he'd wanted to do the night they'd had dinner at the supper club and asked her not to leave.

"Loren, if you don't have to leave right now, I want you to stay a while."

It didn't escape her when his voice dropped an octave and the relaxed look he had was now tensed with a look of want. His voice was husky and sexy and it made her quiver when he said her name with a hint of a seductive undertone. She looked over at him before replying, taking in just how damn sexy he was. She couldn't stop the reaction her body was having just being in his presence again. She didn't make a move, but she didn't settle back down either.

"Loren? Did you hear me?"

"Yes I did, and sure, I'd love to stay a little longer."

"Good. Can I get you anything to drink? I have water, some juices and a few coolers if you'd like one of those."

"I'll take whatever kind of juice you have."

As he got up to grab her a juice from his kitchen, she placed her belongings back on the table and followed him. She tried not to stare, but couldn't help herself as she watched him move about. He was quite a delectable specimen to behold.

No one spoke as he handed her the juice and all was quiet. Silence hung in the air and since he'd asked her to stick around, she hoped he would explain why. Now it seemed neither of them had anything to say. It wasn't the silence that disturbed her as much as the sexual tension in the room. She knew that Mike had to sense it as well. She nervously drank her juice while wondering what to do next.

Mike watched Loren as she drank her juice, afraid to say anything, not sure of what would come out of his mouth. He'd gotten up the nerve to ask her to stay and now what? he thought. He wanted her so bad that if he opened his mouth to say a word, he would spill every thought that was floating around about him and her being naked and sweaty.

Loren couldn't take the silence and the not knowing anymore. She sat her glass down and looked up at him, into those eyes of his that held so much promise and into his handsome face that she wanted to caress with her hands. To keep from doing so, she placed her hands in the back pocket of her jeans and inquired.

"Mike, what's this? What are we doing here?"

She watched as her questions perplexed him, catching him off guard. He had to know that one of them had to say something.   She waited for him to get his thoughts together. His stance looked tranquil, but the expression on his face was one of confusion. He was struggling, that much was obvious.

Mike knew this was it, he either does or the opportunity dies.

"I don't know Loren. I'm trying not to do anything here. I'm trying really hard, but I think I'm losing the battle. I have a problem and I'm not quite sure how to handle it. The problem is you, which is not a bad thing, depending on how you look at it."

Mike looked at her and it was obvious he wasn't choosing the right words. She looked worried. Now he really needed to fix things.

"Can I be honest here?" he asked.

"Yes, I wish you would."

Mike took a deep breath and not holding anything back, he put it all out for her to hear.

"Okay, here it goes. I'm very attracted to you and I have been for a very long time. I can't stop thinking about you and I don't know if that's weird or not for you considering our connection is through my closeness with your brother and your family and we all seem to be one big happy family, but my thoughts about you have nothing to do with family. All I can tell you is that my thoughts when I think of you are not of a sisterly way. I've tried for a long time to ignore these feelings I have for you, but they aren't going away. I play several scenarios over and over in my head about how this could work and every single one of them ends with your brother kicking my ass."

Unbeknownst to him, she knew exactly what he was feeling because she was feeling the same way and had been feeling that way for much longer than he had been, she was sure. After he spoke, she considered what would happen if she was as honest with him as he was with her. Since they were laying everything out, she couldn't let him be the only one out on the limb.

"Mike, what if I told you I have feelings for you as well, that are not brotherly in nature?"

He didn't immediately respond, though he was happy to hear her admission. He thought of a response, but none would solve the problem of the predicament they were in. He still wanted her to know that he understood.

"I would say that we're in serious trouble here. Don't think that I'm shooting down anything that either one of us are feeling here, but this goes way beyond just you and me. Duron is my best friend and my business partner. I love your family as if they were my very own, you know that and I'm not sure they would be receptive to knowing about anything going on as far as the feelings I have for you or the feelings you have for me. I think they expect me to be that older brother figure and nothing more. I know for a fact that Duron would kill me if I ever took action on my feelings for you. It's dangerous territory Loren, yet here we are."

She understood completely what he was saying. She was having the same struggles when it came to what her family would think of any type of connection between them besides friendship.

"Okay Mike, can I be even more honest here?"

Mike merely shook his head yes in response.

"I haven't been able to stop thinking about you since the night we danced. It somehow felt different. It felt sexual and erotic and I wanted to leave because I was feeling out of control. I needed to put some space between us. Then in the car, I really wanted you to kiss me, but somehow I was glad when you didn't, not because I didn't want the kiss, but because I wasn't sure what it would lead to or what I was ready for."

"When did you become this beautiful woman standing in front of me? One day you are this young girl and then I look up and you're this gorgeous woman."

"Mike, with all of the women you run through, I hardly think that you have enough time to focus on me, but it's very flattering of you to say so."

"It's not flattery Loren, it's the truth. Yes, I do date a lot of women, but it's all non-committal and that's mutually agreed upon. That also doesn't mean I don't think of you because I do. I think that you are beautiful and any other man with eyes can see that."

Loren nibbled on her lip, nervously hearing the compliment. She'd often been told that by men, but for some reason, it sounded different coming from Mike and she not only believed him, but she liked hearing him say it.

"I make you nervous Loren? If so, that's not my intent when I compliment you."

"No, you don't make me nervous."

He knew she was lying.

"Loren, you are nibbling on your lips. You do that when you're nervous."

He smiled and she smiled back, liking that he knew her so well.

"Okay, well maybe just a little. It's not you that makes me nervous Mike, it's being around you that makes me nervous. I like you, but I wouldn't want anything to come in between not only your friendship, but the successful business partnership you have with Duron."

He understood what Loren was saying and he was glad that she could relate to how he was feeling.

"So what do you suggest we do here Loren? I don't think this vibe that's developing between us is going to go away. Jase mentioned it to me that night at the restaurant."

Mike's comment about Jase shocked her.

"Jason mentioned what that night?" she asked, shocked.

He couldn't back out now with giving her all of the details.

"He mentioned that he could see something was happening between us and his advice was that I stop it now before all hell broke loose if I acted on what he thought he saw. He's right you know. Knowing my reputation with the ladies, Duron would kick my ass if he knew I had thoughts about his sister, like what he and I have shared over the years about women. You know how he is when it comes to you. He's got shields up and no one passes go or collects two hundred dollars that he doesn't approve of and we both know, it doesn't matter how close friends we are, he knows my lifestyle and nowhere will he see his sister fitting into that."

Loren smiled at his mentioned of the object of the Monopoly game. She looked over at him standing, waiting for her direction. He needed her to take the lead here and walk away because though he obviously wanted her, he didn't want this to become a sour spot and ruin friendships because he couldn't control his libido.

"What do you want to do Mike?"

Mike hesitated before deciding if he should be totally honest with her. He wanted her in the worse way and her being here with him now, knowing how he felt about her and him knowing she felt the same way was more than he could bare. She was looking sexy and desirable and it was taking everything in him to not reach for her, remove every stitch of clothing that kept him from her luscious body and take her right in his kitchen. That's what he really wanted to do, but the head that was thinking logically knew that he should grab Loren's things, hand them to her and walk her to her car as he headed out for a night with the fellas. His other head though, wanted to be buried deep in her lithe body and stay there for the rest of the night. He wish he had time to carefully think of his response but he didn't. She was staring at him, waiting for him to add clarity to the situation. She spoke up before he had a chance to.

"Mike, I'm going to make this very easy for us both and leave. I care about you and the last thing I want is for you to have to grapple with any feelings you have for me and your loyalty to my brother. I have the same struggle and the same loyalty and you know how I feel about Duron. I agree that he would not take kindly to anything happening between us knowing what he knows about your private life with women."

When Mike didn't make a move to respond or react in any way, Loren took a deep breath and moved to get by him to grab her things from the other room and head to her car. When she reached where Mike stood in the doorway, she was about to pass him when he grabbed her lightly around the waist to stop her and leaned down to whisper in her ear.

"I don't want you to go. You asked me what I wanted. Well, what I want is to take you in my room, slowly remove every stitch of clothing you have on and make love to you for the rest of the night. It's all I've been able to think about since I held you in my arms and danced with you.

My mind is so foggy with thoughts of you right now that I really don't care what your brother would think. He could beat me to a pulp, but at least it would be after I've had the chance to hold you in my arms, skin to skin as you scream out my name when you come apart from the pleasure I believe we both would experience, beyond anything either of us has experienced before. That's how right I feel I am about the connection between us. You asked me what I want? That's what I want Loren. I want you, right now. Can I have you?"

She was speechless. Mike's voice never went above a whisper and the soft spoken words made her body moist in the best way. Never had words spoken by any man had such an impact on not just her mind, but also her body. She wanted him with a desire she had never felt before. It wasn't just the words he spoke, but it was the man saying them. This was the man she'd had more than a few wet dreams about over the years. Now here she was a woman, standing in his home, listening to him tell her how much he wanted her. She knew how much she wanted him and there was no denying it. Neither one of them could deny anything.

When Loren didn't move forward or turn to look at him he didn't know what to think. He knew she was thinking about what he'd just said to her and he knew he had to give her time to think it through. He was glad that in the midst of all of this, she wasn't running for the door, but giving it some serious thought.

"Loren, are you going to answer me? What if I asked you just for this one night? Could you give me that? Could you give us that? I know you want me as much as I want you and I think we both know what could happen if anyone found out, so I'm offering you a night of pure pleasure and no one has to know. That is if that's what you want. I don't want to cause problems or confusion around us, but I can't deny how much I want you. What about you, huh? What I don't want is for you to think that you are just another woman I'm bedding for the night because that's not it at all; I want you. I really want you and I'm willing to take you any way that you are willing to offer. I'm not putting you in a group with other women I've been with for one night stands or on any other casual level. My feelings for you go a little deeper than that. I have to let you take the lead here. I need to know that whatever happens between us, you're going to be okay with. I don't want it to lead to problems outside of this condo. Tell me what you want, Loren and whatever it is, I swear I will abide by it and if you want to leave, it won't have an impact on our friendship or our ability to work together. I respect you too much to let anything interfere with that."

This time he stopped talking and waited for her response. He would respect whatever she decided. They remained standing with him against the doorway with his arm holding her around the waist. The next move had to be hers. The choice, the decision had to be Loren's. He looked at her as she exhaled then turned to look up at him. She said very few words, but it was enough.

"I want you Mike."

Chapter 7

This was it, Mike thought. No turning back now. He had put it out there and Loren had put the seal on how the evening would play out. Rather than speak and break the moment, he gave into the desire that he had been holding on to. He turned Loren completely around so that her body was up against his as it had been the night when they were dancing. He reached down, slid her hair back off of her face so that he could caress her cheek. As he did so, he braced her chin in his hand and drew her face closer to his. Neither of them closed their eyes as he brushed a soft kiss across her lips first once, then twice before going in a third time for a mind numbing kiss that spoke volumes about how much they were starving for each other. He didn't let the kiss go on forever. If things went the way he hoped, they had all night to kiss and do anything else they wanted.

"You are so beautiful. Are you sure you're okay with this? I don't want to pressure you simply because I want you so bad. I need you to want this too."

Loren didn't answer him. She just leaned closer, giving

him a sign that she was all in.

He took that hint, leaned down and took Loren's lips with a masterful kiss for a second time. The kiss was filled with passion and fire from the many nights he'd gone to bed thinking about doing this very thing with her. He put his all into the kiss by treating her lips as if they were as precious as porcelain. He nipped, he sucked, he tugged, he pulled and then he dipped into her mouth full force pouring everything into it, letting her know what was in store for them. When he reached down and pulled her even closer while devouring her mouth, his body lit up like a fuse when she reached up to wrap her arms around his neck, as far as they would go.

Loren couldn't think straight. She'd never been kissed so intimately or so thoroughly before. She tried to give as much as she was getting from him, letting him know that he should have no doubt that she wanted to be with him as much as he wanted to be with her, even if it was only for tonight.

Being this close to him she could feel his strong chest through his shirt as it rubbed against her now very sensitive nipples. She had no doubt they were erect because the lace of her demi-bra rubbing back and forth was giving off an incredible, erotic feeling. She was ready and she wanted more; she needed more. Mike must have sensed her need because he reached down with little effort, picked her up and walked with her in his arms towards his bedroom without breaking the kiss. She was glad because she had no plans of letting go of his lips even if he tried. They felt and tasted too good.

Mike was devouring her lips and the more he kissed her the more responsive she became to him and he loved it. He went from tugging on her lips to pulling on her tongue. His hands were roaming all over her body as he got acquainted with the feel of her. He was glad when he finally made it to his bedroom still holding Loren in his arms while plundering her mouth over and over, moaning to let her know how turned on he was by her.

The kiss was like water or air to her. It was no longer just a want, but was now a need. She wanted to crawl into his mouth with her whole body and stay there. His kiss was filled with so much promise of what was in store for her for the night and she couldn't wait.

Mike grabbed her behind and pulled it closer to him so that she could feel how much he wanted her. When she started grinding into him, he was jolted with a need so strong for her that if he didn't soon slow things down, this was going to be over quickly. He could stand, kissing her forever, but he needed to get inside of her. That's where he wanted to be. He'd had dreams about what it would feel like to have her arms and legs wrapped around his body as he made love to her over and over.

He lowered Loren to the floor and reached for the two tops she had on, pulling them both over her head at the same time. He wasn't surprised to see the bright green lace bra that covered her luscious mounds.

Her breasts were calling out to him and he answered right away by lowering the cups and taking one of her nipples between his teeth, while he reached around to unhook it with a quick flick that would win a world record for how fast he was able to unsnap it. He never stopped looking at her as he flung the bra to someplace in the room. It didn't matter to him because he simply needed it out of his way.

Without hesitation, he reached down for the snap on her jeans as he used his tongue to caress her collarbone and placed soft kisses down toward her breasts. Her breasts were high and plump with large dark nipples. He sucked the other breasts in his mouth, making sure they both got equal attention. He was rewarded with the sweetest sound of pleasure released from Loren's lips. He knew she must have been waiting for him to caress her like this. Her reaction to him was just what he needed. He needed to know that he was making her feel good.

He had spent many nights thinking about her and wondering what it would be like to be here with her like he was tonight. Now he knew and he wouldn't want to be any other place than right here. As he continued making love to her breasts with his mouth, he finally unsnapped her jeans and slowly slid down the zipper. Where he would have then reached up from her zipper to slide the jeans down her legs, he detoured and instead, reached his hand down inside the opening of her jeans, right into her panties. He pushed his hand further and further down until he reached the nub that was hard and waiting for his caress.

On his first touch, Loren almost collapsed from the overpowering feeling he was eliciting from her. With the assault his tongue was giving her breasts and now the invasion of his fingers on her most sensitive spot, she was already getting close to climaxing and they had just begun. She couldn't figure out which pleasure to focus on. Both assaults were pleasure beyond anything she had ever felt before. She thought that she would surely die when Mike starting kissing his way back up from her breasts to her neck then to her ear. She was breathing so hard, that in any other situation, someone might think that she were about to have a heart attack.

"I see you're ready for me," he whispered in her ear right before sticking his tongue in for a quick stroke.

Loren couldn't breathe. She certainly couldn't speak to respond. She had no words, so she just moaned louder and louder, using her sounds to respond.

"I love how you respond to me," Mike said as he continued stroking her over-sensitive nub over and over again. Loren could feel her juices as they began coating his fingers as they derived more and more pleasure from her. She wanted to squeeze her legs together to keep them there, but she didn't want to hinder him from what he was doing to her.

"Does this feel good, Loren?"

A moan in response was all she could utter. All verbal speech was beyond reach.

"Mm hmm," she murmured.

In between licks of her ear, Mike whispered, "All night tonight baby, I intend to make you feel just like this. I want to know what turns you on. I want you to tell me all the things you've ever wanted to have done to your body so that I can pleasure you, not only the way I want, but the way you want your body pleasured."

The whispering, the licking and the stroking was almost too much for Loren. Her body felt ready to explode and this is all before either of them were fully undressed.

Mike could tell by Loren's reaction to what his hand was doing to her that she was close to the edge. He slowed things down a bit because this was not the position he wanted her to be in when she first crested. He removed his hand from her panties to remove the rest of her clothing.

Once he had Loren standing before him completely naked, he quickly removed every stitch of clothing he had on as well.

Loren's vision was sort of hazy because she was so stimulated. She watched as Mike removed his clothing and saw that he was very long, very thick and very much aroused. His penis was so veiny that the way they were protruding looked painful, but she knew it wasn't. She was happy she was having this type of an effect on him. She had no doubt that he would bring her pleasure all night long. He had the kind of penis that was meant for doing just that. She thought back to all of the dreams she had about him and what he would look like and they were all correct. No wonder women couldn't get enough of him. She had not had many lovers, but the couple that she did have, didn't even come close to comparing in size.

Mike reached into his night stand to withdraw a condom, placing it on the bed. After doing so, he turned his attention back to Loren. He didn't want to wait any longer to give them both the enjoyment they sought. He reached down, picked her up, curving her legs around his waist. He turned her around so that he could lay her on her back on the bed. When he did so, he came down on top of her, keeping her legs wrapped around his waist. He went straight for her breasts knowing she love the attention he paid them.

Loren ground her body into his wanting him to know she was more than ready for him. She closed her eyes and focused on the pure delight of being with him. It was more than she could have ever imagined and she had a vivid imagination. She and her *Bullet*, which she had named Mike, on many nights did nothing to compare to having the real thing.

Mike slid slowly down Loren's body until his tongue met the hooded cover that housed the nub that he needed to get to. He loved that she was as smooth as the day she was born except for one thing strip of hair that he slid his tongue back and forth across.

Now he was ready to turn it up and turn it up he did. He used his tongue to stroke her nub this time. He flicked it back and forth and added a little pressure as he did so knowing it would drive her crazy and judging by her reaction, it did to his delight.

He continued his ministrations as Loren reached down and grabbed a hold of his head. He could tell she was close and he wanted her to come apart in his arms just like this. He looked up to see how beautiful she looked in the throes of passion, about to let go. With long swipes of his tongue, he knew the moment Loren went over the edge. She ground hard into his mouth and moaned loud, followed by a loud scream of pleasure as she pulled as much from him as he poured it onto her. Her orgasm went on and on and still he didn't let up. He gave and gave, until her spasms started to subside.

While she came down some from the high of her orgasm, she watched as Mike made his way back up her body, kissing a path along the way until he reached her mouth where he focused his attention.

Mike had been with a lot of women, but never had one been as responsive to him as Loren. It may be that he never really paid as much attention as he was paying with Loren. He was always an attentive lover, but with Loren, it really meant something and he wanted to savor every single moment.

Loren could not believe how strong her orgasm was. It normally took her a lot longer to reach that point unless she was pleasuring herself. Mike was a master at what he was doing and she loved every bit of it. Her body felt relaxed and well sexed and she knew that this was only the beginning.

Mike was anything, but traditional when it came to sex. He loved the missionary position as much as the next person, but he loved to explore. He wanted to take Loren in a different way. He reached for the condom, placed it on and rolled Loren to her side so that he could spoon her. He continued to kiss her on her neck and moved down to her shoulder while lifting her right leg and placing it over his thigh. He let his hands roam all over her body, arousing her once again.

"Baby, I bet you feel as good as you taste," Mike said as he took his time sliding into her body from the spooning position. Loren was pretty tight so he had to take his time entering her body a little at a time, allowing her tight sheath to adjust to his size. He had to grit his teeth to keep from going all the way in on his first push. With Loren being wet and ready for him again, it made his entry easier and bearable for him, but he wanted to be sure she felt pleasure and not pain. The feeling of being inside of her was intense and he had to remind himself to breathe.

When he was finally completely inside of her, he slowly slid back out while continuing to caress her shoulder, her back and her neck with kisses. He was secretly praying he could prolong this pleasure for them both, but he wasn't sure he could. Being with her this way surpassed any dream he'd ever hd.

Loren was in heaven. She felt herself pushing back

towards Mike as he pushed forward into her. He had set a rhythm that was easy for her to follow. They started out with a slow grind until he picked up the pace, surging into her body faster. She reached down to grab hold of his hand that had covered her breast. She held on as he rocked into her harder and harder, giving it to her the way she liked without her having to tell him. Every time he entered her body, he would hit his mark and a burst of electricity would shoot through her from her feet all the way up her body. She could once again, feel her body getting close to reaching its peak and she started racing to get to it. She already knew what it was going to be like and she wanted that feeling again with him.

As Mike's strokes became longer and harder, the sound of flesh smacking against flesh turned her on even more.

Mike continued pushing into her over and over and when he reached down to stroke her with his fingers, she was done. Spasm after spasm rocked her body she rode the wave as surged through every fiber of her being. In her sex laden haze, she could tell Mike was reaching his climax as well. She continued her strokes back into him, harder and harder to help prolong his pleasure as well. She felt it when he grabbed on to her hip to hold her steady as he reached his crowning moment, grunting his release into her neck, never letting up on his powerful strokes. They continued like this until they were both wrought of all energy.

As they came down from the high, Mike stayed connected to Loren intimately as he held her close to him. He never wanted to let her go. Out the window flew his idea of being with her this one time. He knew he mentioned having this one night with her, but after what they had just experienced, there was no way he was going to be able to settle for just one night.

"Loren, are you okay? he asked after he gained the ability to speak again.

"I'm fine. In fact I am wonderful and you were incredible," she said as she turned around so that they were facing each other.

He looked so handsome and she couldn't resist stealing another powerful kiss from him. Through the kiss they held on to each other as if neither ever wanted to let go. He felt so right in her arms.

Mike saw no signs of regret on Loren's face and he looked. He didn't want an incredible moment to turn bad because the aftermath had settled in. Still, he needed to know.

"Are we okay?" he finally asked.

Loren knew he wanted to be sure she wasn't going to have any regrets about what they just did.

"Mike, we're fine. I'm a big girl. I wanted this as much as you did and I have no regrets."

She saw relief on his handsome face.

"I'm glad. I don't want tonight marred by any second thoughts, after the fact. Are you hungry?"

"I'm starving," she replied.

"I'm going to hit the bathroom then I'll go round us up something to eat from the kitchen."

"Okay. You definitely worked up my appetite," she said, laughing.

Mike smiled.

"I aim to please baby."

He leaned over to give her one last smooch before going to dispose of the condom and feeding another hunger they both had; for food.

~~

He came back from the kitchen with fresh fruit, cheese and salami. Loren's stomach growled the minute she saw it. He placed the tray across her lap, turned on some quiet, slow music and joined her on the bed. He watched as she attacked the food like a starving woman.

He laughed at her.

"Hungry a little maybe?"

Loren almost choked trying to eat and laugh.

"Come on now. The one thing you know about me is I love to eat."

She grabbed a strawberry and reached to feed it to him. He grabbed the strawberry along with her fingers with his teeth. That act hit Loren with thoughts of fruit and sex and all they could do. Her body's reaction to that gesture showed the affect he had on her.

"Mmm, you taste good mixed in with some strawberries. I'll have to remember that for the future," he whispered.

Loren didn't miss that his comment meant that he intended to have more than the one night that they had decided on earlier.

"There's going to be a future beyond tonight between us where you'll need strawberries?" she inquired.

When Mike didn't immediately respond Loren began to wonder if he didn't mean to say it at all.

He looked at her wondering why he'd blurted that out. He didn't want to scare her away, but he also wanted more than just one night with her. He reached over, removed the tray from her lap and decided to table that discussion for another time. He had other ideas on his mind of how to occupy the time they had left and he didn't want to waste it talking.

He removed the blanket that was covering her and slid her down so that her body laid flush under his.

"Spend the entire night with me," he asked, hoping she wanted it as much as he did.

Loren reached up, pulled Mike down on top of her, close enough so that their lips were almost touching. She snaked her tongue out to lick his lips seductively.

"Why Mike, what will we do with all of the hours left if I spend the entire night?"

Mike smiled at her humor. He reached over to his night stand, withdrew another condom and replied, "I have the most interesting concepts for the rest of the night that I'd like to share with you. I would tell you all about them, but I'd rather show you."

Loren was thrilled when he proceeded to do just that.

Chapter 8

Loren woke startled to discover she was in a bed that didn't feel like her own and she wasn't alone. It only took her a few seconds to remember where she was and who she was with. She shifted slightly and felt a wonderful ache between her legs and everything became crystal clear. She was at Mike's condo, currently in his bed. They had spent the last couple of hours indulging in the best sex of her life. She thought back over how she had come to be in his bed when she felt a very light kiss on her shoulder. She looked back over her shoulder into his dark and her heart melted.

"Hi," was all Loren could get out.

Instead of saying hello back, Mike leaned down and placed the softest kiss on her lips. She responded as if it were the most natural thing in the world to be here with him like this. When he'd drank his fill from the kiss, he leaned back on his elbow and said hello back.

"Hi yourself. How are you feeling?"

"I'm feeling wonderful," she declared.

"I can tell it's still dark outside so it's not morning yet.

What time is it?" she asked while leaning into a much needed stretch.

"It's about four in the morning."

"Oh wow. You missed your evening with your friends. I'm sorry for interrupting your plans."

Mike loved how caring and sensitive Loren was. Those were traits he had come to enjoy about her over the years.

"You didn't interrupt anything. I wouldn't want to be any other place other than here with you. I hope you feel the same way."

She turned all the way around so that they were now face to face, snuggling. She felt comfortable being in bed with Mike.

"I am exactly where I want to be right now."

"Only right now Loren?"

"Right now is what we have Mike. You know as well as I do that this can only be right now."

He didn't respond, but decided to take advantage of the fact that he had a gorgeous, sexy and most definitely gloriously naked woman in his bed. He leaned over to get another deep, searing kiss. Before too long the kiss turned scorching hot and he moved to completely cover her body with his as he took the kiss deeper and deeper. As Loren responded to the onslaught of his kiss, Mike felt his body harden. He couldn't seem to get enough of her.

Loren felt the change in Mike the moment he took her mouth in a kiss that had her responding to him as if it were the last kiss they would share. She got the feeling he initiated the kiss to avoid having the discussion they both knew needed to happen. She would eventually be getting up and leaving and what they had shared over the past few hours would be all that they could share. Too much was at stake to continue. For now she would let him forget about the inevitable and enjoy the moment.

Loren leaned up into the kiss as Mike pressed down harder on her with his entire body. His body hardened with anticipation above her of what was to come once again. She reached out and grabbed the long, hard and extremely aroused length of his penis. She held on and stroked his length first up then down.

"Loren, baby your hand feels so good. Don't stop," he crooned into her mouth, between kisses.

"Now, why would I stop? This feels just as good to me as it does to you" she sighed into his mouth.

"Yes, yes, yes," was all Mike could say. He just wanted to feel. He could stay like this forever with her. As she continued to stroke him, she pushed forward, tilting until he was flat on his back, allowing her to crawl over him, again not breaking the kiss or the intimate grip she had on his penis. She felt like a she-devil with all the power. She wanted to pleasure him as much as he had been pleasuring her. She felt so free and comfortable with Mike that she knew that whatever they shared intimately, he would be open for. She had not always felt this free when it came to intimacy, but he made her feel like this. She moved so that her legs straddled his body and continued to stroke him and focus on his face that expressed pure delight at what she was doing. She watched as he closed his eyes and she knew that he was completely focused on the sensations she was drawing from him. She watched as he reached out blindly for her.

"No, no," Loren said, teasingly. "It's my turn to make you half-crazy with lust."

"You mean your turn to tease me don't you," he said still

not opening his eyes.

"Just lay back and enjoy big boy," she said to him and to his penis.

She leaned down and placed kisses across his chest, taking first one nipple then the other between her teeth. When she tugged, she felt his body leap up off of the bed.

"You are torturing me," he said through clenched teeth.

"You haven't experienced torture yet," she said, with a hint of something sinister in her voice.

Loren felt empowered, she felt sexy and she felt adventurous. She was about to do something she had never done before. She wanted to pleasure him with her mouth just as he had done for her. The desire to taste him had become too overwhelming to ignore. She slid further down his body until her face was even with that part of him that she wanted and needed.

"I can feel your wetness on my leg Loren. Come up here and let me take care of that for you," he said very breathy, proving how stimulated he was.

He reached blindly for her again.

"Not this time baby. I want to see how wet I can make you for me," she said slyly.

Loren kept her eyes planted directly on his because she wanted to see his reaction the moment she took him in her mouth.

Before she did, she wanted to drive him crazy. She first licked her tongue out to caress the head of his penis. She licked all around it as he continued to moan and grind through the pleasure. She had never done this before, but had seen it done by watching some pretty raunchy movies over the years. How else was a girl to learn, she thought.

When Mike began to grind up into her mouth, she

continued with her very slow ministrations. After licking around the head, she stroked up and down his entire length with her tongue, tasting the salty, yet sweetness of him.

Mike thought that any minute he was going to have a stroke. Never had he felt such pleasure before and she was drawing his out very slowly. He was a big fan of oral sex, but he never thought he would feel like he was floating. Being with Loren was everything he thought it would be and right now she was giving him pleasure beyond anything he had ever experienced before and he knew he'd experienced plenty. This was different because it was Loren and he needed more.

"More baby, I need more," he moaned.

Loren didn't reply, she just gave him more. After her final lick up, she opened her mouth wider to receive him. She knew there was no way she would be able to take him all in, but she was willing to take as much as she could, giving him as much as she could. As she began pleasuring him her own level of arousal was escalating. She had no idea pleasuring a man this way could bring her just as much satisfaction. Loren looked up at Mike just as he opened his eyes, glazed over with pure lust. Her pulse quickened as she watched him try to contain the orgasm she knew was right in his reach. She didn't want him to fight it. She increased her motions and j just when she thought he was on the brink, he reached down and pulled her body up with his. He took her mouth in a kiss that had her teetering on the edge. She was a little disappointed that he didn't let her finish.

"Why did you stop me?" she asked.

"I needed to. As good as you were making me feel, and

believe me it was feeling really good, I want to be inside you. I want and need to feel you."

He kissed her tenderly hoping she'd understand that he didn't stop her because he didn't like it. He stopped her because he loved it, but he also loved the way her body gripped his like a glove and he needed to feel that right now.

While he explored her mouth, Loren reached over and grabbed another condom from the night stand. She broke the kiss long enough to roll the condom on him and rose to slide down on his girth. This was also new for her. She was not the most experienced lover, but she loved trying new things and throughout the night, she and Mike had done just that. He allowed her to do whatever she wanted and anything she wanted him to do to her, he quickly obliged. They gasped in unison as she slid down onto him. The feeling was extreme and her body was already sensitized that it didn't take long for her to climax. She used her inner muscles to grip Mike tight as she rode him that it didn't take him long either.

Mike knew it was over the moment he felt the vice like grip Loren's body had on his. He held on to her hips, guiding her as she rode him while he entered her over and over. They rode out their explosive orgasms together.

The roar that escaped his lips hit him like a tsunami. It washed over him quicker than he expected and it seemed to go on forever.

Loren never stopped riding out her pleasure. He wanted to give her much more. While in the current throws of passion, he reached down to stroke her intimately, even though he knew she had just climaxed. He wanted her to do it again, just for him.

"Again, for me baby," he whispered. "Again."

Loren never opened her eyes. She continued astride him.

"I don't think I can," she uttered, still not stopping.

"Yes you can. Do it for me baby. Come on, I feel the need in your body," he encouraged.

He stroked her until he could feel her building up again. He could feel her reaching for that precipice once more exactly like he wanted her to. If this was all they were going to have, he wanted everything from her. He set out to give her a night she would never forget and he planned to do just that. He never wanted her to forget what it was like to make love with him.

When she was finally done, she collapsed on his body like dead weight. She couldn't move and Mike didn't make a move to move her from on top of him. They stayed in that position until they were both able to finally speak.

"I have never ever done that before. Tonight with you has been filled with a night of firsts for me, the greatest is being able to be with you."

"You are incredible," he replied.

He wanted to say more, but his mind was racing with how to convince her that this can't be it for them. Once Loren slid from his body to the bed, he pulled her closer to him so that she was snug up against him. He pulled the blanket over them and no further words were said as they both slipped into a deep slumber.

Neither Mike nor Loren were asleep as daylight broke out across the sky. They lay together spooning with Mike close behind her. Loren could lay like this forever, but she knew it wasn't possible. Sadness settled over her at the thought that she needed to get up and leave after waiting so many years to be in his arms.

She turned so that she could face him.

"Mike. I'm going to get ready to go. Thank you for an incredible night. I enjoyed being with you. This was better than any dream I ever had about you."

"I enjoyed being with you also."

Neither moved to get up. They continued gazing at and caressing each other. Mike knew they were thinking the same thing, that being together felt right. It was as if they were meant to be together and not just for one night. He figured Loren was waiting for him to say something else, but the words would not come. He knew that she should leave, but he just couldn't let her. Not yet. Not until he said his peace.

Loren moved to extricate herself from the way her body was entwined with his. When she stood, she felt the loss of the close connection to Mike. Could she really just walk away like they didn't spend the most incredible night in each other arms? She grabbed her clothes that were still lying all over the floor and made her way to the connecting bathroom to get dressed. She rushed, not wanting Mike to see the despair on her face at having to leave as if nothing had happened.

After Loren entered the bathroom, Mike sat up on the side of the bed, distraught himself about the current circumstance. He had finally made love to Loren for what was to be the first and last time and it wasn't sitting well with him. He got up to grab a pair of jeans to put on while he thought. He could not just let Loren leave as if nothing happened between them. How could he, from this point forward, look at her and not want to be with her? While she got dressed, he went to the kitchen for coffee to clear his head. There was no way this would be the one and only time he could be with her this way. The evening before, he thought that once they were able to get each other out of their systems by spending the night together, that it would be enough. That was exactly the Mike she expected him to be because that was the Mike she knew him to be. He agreed that it was the Mike that he normally was, but this was different. He didn't just want to bed Loren as he'd done with other women, he wanted to spend more time getting to know her on a deeper level and figuring out why, even after the numerous number of times he had made love to her through the night, he still wanted her just as much as he did before he ever touched her.

Loren was thinking too hard while taking a shower. She had no idea being with Mike would have this much of an impact on her.

After her shower and once she was dressed, she entered the kitchen to find Mike at the counter, pouring coffee for him and her.

"Sugar and cream in your coffee?" he asked.

"Just a little cream, thanks."

He passed her the cup and marveled at how incredibly sexy she looked early in the morning. No one said a word as they both drank their coffee. They knew the inevitable had to happen. It was a matter of who spoke it first. They weren't even looking at each other.

"Look at me Loren," he said softly, tapping into the solemn mood that had settled over the room.

She look up at him slowly.

"I'm going to say what I think we both are thinking here because I can't let you leave without having this discussion. The elephant in the room warrants it."

A Designed Affair

Loren nodded in agreement because she was feeling the same way. She knew exactly what he was talking about.

"I felt more than just a sexual connection with you last night. I don't know about you, but I'm not sure I can just walk away from you and continue on as if nothing has happened, all for the sake of family and friends. I can't begin to tell you how long I have wanted you. I don't know how to move forward without those closest to us finding out. I, for one, am willing to deal with the consequences, but I don't want to cause any drama in your family and certainly not with your brother. I know that my desire for you did not lessen now that we have slept together. I didn't get you out of my system. If nothing, you are wedged even further in it. It's taken my want for you, my desire for you, a lot higher and much deeper. Can you honestly just walk away from me now?"

Loren's words were caught in her throat. She was afraid to express how she really felt. If she did, she knew it would give Mike the ammunition he needed to come up with a way to continue what they shared last night and as much as she still wanted him, she couldn't risk what would happen to Mike personally and professionally because they couldn't stay away from each other. She did, however want him to know something.

"Mike, when I was younger and I first met you, you were just another one of my brother's friends. I think I was a tomboy back then and not really all that into boys. I had grown up with three older brothers and all I wanted to do was be like them. My parents were so happy with I got away from them and went to Spellman and finally let go of my tomboyish ways. It was in those years when I would see you occasionally that I started to see you differently. I would have dreams about you and I used to imagine kissing you and being held by you. When I saw you at my graduate school graduation celebration all I could think about was how much I wanted you. Being with you last night was more than and better than any dream of you that I could ever have. What I'm faced with now is the light of day. With the light of day brings reality and the reality is, I enjoyed the night with you, but there is too much at stake for this to be anything beyond what happened between us last night. I know it and you know it."

Her words were first met with silence. When she thought he wouldn't respond, he spoke up.

"I know what you're trying to say and I understand. You have to admit we had some kind of connection all night long and not just during the sex. We have really connected Loren and I don't want to stop with last night."

"Mike, one thing I know for a fact is that this," Loren made her point by pointing back and forth from her to him, "is not going beyond this moment. Do you have any idea the impact this could have on your relationship with my brother? Not that Duron doesn't love you like a brother, but he also knows you better than a brother. He's knows your reputation with the ladies and we both know how overprotective he is of me. He wouldn't be happy about anything between you and I and you two have been best friends since college and business partners for a few years now, building a multi-million dollar business together. He may love you like a brother, but he won't be accepting of you and I. You know that just as well as I do."

He wasn't giving up yet because though he heard the words coming out of her mouth, he knew she didn't want things to end any more than he did. She was just scared.

"Loren, listen. We can't live for your brother or anyone else. This is about you and me. Do you tell your brother who to and not to date? I know it's not the same because you are the sister, but the issue is that you are a grown woman and you can date whom you choose. So can I, and I want us to explore where we can go with this."

Loren looked at him not knowing what to really say, but needing to say something.

"Mike, I loved being with you last night, really I did. I can't tell you how much. It meant everything to me, but if we are both being really honest here, I don't think you are truly ready. I don't want to change who you are. I know being involved with one woman is not your thing, but it's what I expect when I'm involved."

She saw Mike try to cut in to explain himself.

"Before you cut me off, let me finish. There is a lot at stake here. Not just the issue with my family or my brother not being accepting of you and me. There is also that fact that I don't want to be hurt and I think you'd hurt me. I think that I would have such high expectations that I don't think you're ready for."

"How do you know that if you aren't open to giving anything a try? I would never set out to deliberately hurt you Loren and you have to know that about me," he explained.

"Mike, I know you would not deliberately do that. That doesn't mean it wouldn't happen."

She could see he was getting frustrated and she needed to leave to clear her head a little. She looked at him and all she wanted to do was crawl back in bed with him.

"Thank you for a wonderful evening, Mike. I'm going to leave now before I forget all I just said to convince myself, and you, that this is not a good idea and relive last night by going after what's behind that zipper."

Loren's gaze followed her words to the bulge that was becoming obvious behind the zipper in his pants. As her gaze moved higher to his gorgeous face, the temptation was getting to her so she turned and headed for the door. She could hear him following her and closing the gap between them before she could get out of the door. As she reached for the handle, he was right up against her back slowly pressing her up against the door, preventing her from opening it. Her breath quickened as he leaned down and whispered close to her ear.

"Loren, this is not over. You've made your case and again, I do respect that, but my respect for it doesn't mean I agree with it. I want to see you again. Just think about it."

He then did something that she wasn't expecting. He placed the sweetest, softest kiss on the back of her neck, but not just a kiss. It was a kiss that started with the feel of his lips on her neck then he snaked his tongue out and lightly licked the tiny hairs on the back of her neck setting her body on fire. In a few moments, she knew she would be unable to resist him. She didn't want to fight him. She wanted to turn around and get lost in the feel of him.

Mike knew he needed to stop because he sensed the struggle she was going through. He was pushing her and he didn't want to do that. He could sense her inner battle. He stepped back so that she could leave. Once he did so, she turned, smiled up at him, opened the door and left.

Loren was experiencing the longest elevator ride in her life. Everything bone in her body wanted to push the button that would take her back up to the penthouse level.

She wanted to fling Mike's door open, throw herself in his arms and kiss him until he took her back to bed. She fought the temptation and kept her hands in her pocket, not reaching for the buttons.

She was busy reminiscing about the night she spent with Mike, when the elevator door opened, she didn't see Duron walking towards her across the garage of the building as she headed toward her car.

"Loren? What are you doing here so early in the morning?" her brother asked.

She was caught off guard and didn't know how to explain why she was in the building at such an ungodly hour. She played it off.

"Hey D. The better question is, why are you here?"

Duron looked at her like she was a foreigner. She knew he was a workaholic.

"Oh right, you spend way too much time in the office on weekends. Or, wait, is this you coming in from a late night of creeping? Actually, don't answer that. I don't even want to know."

"Lo, you still didn't answer my question. What did you do, spend the night at my condo last night? I know they delivered all of the art yesterday."

Saved!! Loren thought.

"Yeah, I did. The art looks great too. It took me a while to get things exactly like I wanted and I think you'll be pleased. It was getting late when we finished up so I stayed here rather than head back to my place. You know you have the best snack food" she said.

Loren could see he bought it with no problem since he knew that she had a habit of making herself at home at his condo just as she did at his home out in Buckhead.

"I swear I don't know why you don't weigh a few hundred pounds because all you do is eat."

"Yeah well, I'm surprised you have any life at all since you're always working, so I guess we both have personal issues we need to work out. I'm leaving because I have a lot to do today. Let me know what you think of the new décor."

Loren gave her brother one last hug and made her way toward her car.

"I'll call you later big brother."

"Wait, Loren. Did you run into Mike while you were here? The guys were expecting him last night and I tried to call him, but got no answer."

"Oh, yeah, I saw him last night when I arrived. Maybe he made other plans or something. She didn't add more, but simply left before Duron asked her any more questions.

Chapter 9

It had been over a week since Mike had seen Loren following the night they spent together. He'd called her a few times and they had actually spoken once about some designing ideas. He'd also let her know that he would be flying out to California to get a grip on the business side of things. He asked her if she wanted to accompany him so that she could see the house and get pictures of the rooms. She was more than excited about the chance to do so. He agreed to make the travel arrangements for her since he would already have his assistant making his arrangements. It was on the tip of his tongue to tell her that he missed her, but he didn't want to put any pressure on her. They would, however, have to deal with the issue between them much sooner than later. For now, he would allow her to have her space. He needed to get himself ready for his meeting with Duron in order to prepare for his trip to the west coast. He grabbed what he needed and met Duron in the conference room.

"So things are pretty much set. I'll be heading to California at the end of the month. The lawyers have looked over the new contracts and everything is a go. I signed my copy this morning. I'm going to leave them in Tyrone's office today so make sure you get them from him this week," Mike said to Duron.

"How is everything going with Taija?" Mike asked. He knew that they had been seeing each other for a minute now.

Mike could tell by the big smile his friend was sporting at the mention of the name of the woman he was currently seeing so he knew things must be pretty good.

"Man she is incredible and she's definitely the total package. We're having dinner tonight. She's the first woman in a long time that I'm enjoying and it's not just about sex. Imagine that huh?"

Mike faked having a heart attack.

"Whoa, is a true player losing his status up in here or what? Did I hear you correctly?"

Duron laughed at Mike's snide comment about his prowess with the ladies.

"Hey man, I didn't say anything about all that. I just said, I like her. Don't read anything else into that. From one player to another, you know I'm still a card carrying member."

Mike shook his head at Duron. They were definitely too close. They knew too much about each other.

"Loren told me she talked to you about the work you wanted her to do. Why don't you have her also look into the interior design of the office building as well? The temporary space that we'll be using will need a major interior overhaul. She'll be back and forth anyway working on your house so she can kill two birds."

"That's a great idea; I can do that. She's planning to fly

out with me at the end of the month to get her first look at the house anyway. I'll give her a call this evening about it and give her a heads up on the plans for the office."

"You may want to try her tomorrow. She has a date tonight or something."

Mike's back stiffened when he heard Duron mention his sister being out on a date with someone.

"A date huh? Who's she seeing?"

"I don't know man. Some guy she met not too long ago or something. I think originally she and Taija were supposed to hang out or something tonight. Taija said Loren backed out because she had a date which is why she was now free to have dinner with a brother!"

"Does anybody know this guy Loren's going out with?"

"I tried to get Loren to tell me when I called her this morning. She was all closed mouthed about it giving me a speech about being too overprotective and her being a grown woman and all. I know one thing, he better be on the up and up and treat her right or he'll have me to answer to. She hasn't had the best of luck with relationships. The last guy she dated seriously almost ended up on the other side of my fists if it had not been for my brothers who rescued him."

"I remember that. He was a real jerk."

"Yeah, he tried to play my baby sister and man I was about to be all over him. I swear when I saw the tears Loren was crying for that fool and how red her face was from crying so much, I was ready to kill. Men these days are not good enough for my sister. I know I'm not one to talk because I've been a dog most of my adult days, but still that's my sister. I don't want her getting involved with a man anything like how we are. I'm not saying we disrespect women or anything because we don't, but we like to play around and I don't want my sister played with."

Mike was caught off guard by Duron's comment.

"Whoa, what do you mean a man like me?" Mike said with a defensive laced response.

"Mike, I'm not trying to be insulting, but seriously. If you had a sister, would you want her involved with any guy who didn't know how to take relationships seriously? I'm just saying, I don't want my little sister being a notch on someone's bed post. I'm not saying guys like us are the scum of the earth or anything, but when I picture my sister with someone, it's with a guy who I can trust to not step out on her or who is willing to commit to her. She deserves better than that. You get what I'm saying?"

Mike had to admit he did get it, but he knew now was not the time to plead his case as a good guy to Duron. He wanted to know more about this guy Loren was going out with. She never mentioned she was seeing anyone. Of course, she didn't have to mention that to him. They weren't seeing each other.

"I'll wait and give her a call tomorrow then. I don't want to disturb her date night," Mike said, with a negative emphasis on the word date.

"I tried to get her to tell me where she was going. You know her, she wouldn't tell me. She thinks I'd show up to check this dude out. I think her and Taija planned it so that I'd be busy with Taija tonight to keep me from showing up. Taija let it slip that she was going to be at Jason's supper club. I promised her I would not be showing up and ruining her evening by grilling this dude like the protective brother that I am."

Mike now wanted to change the subject. The more he

thought of Loren being out with someone, the madder he seemed to be getting. He changed the conversation back to work.

"One last thing before we break; I did hire a new assistant today. Of those I interviewed, I hired that Chad guy. He's a senior at Morehouse and I think he'll make a great addition to the staff. He'll be able to really help you guys out while I'm back and forth between coasts. I'm going to get him in here starting before I head to California at the end of the month. I'll send him to human resources this week to get all of his paperwork done and the background check completed so that he can start as soon as possible. I have a lot for him to do."

Duron was happy to hear this.

"Sounds good man. We are interviewing a few interns this week and next week I believe. I'm hoping a few will pan out after graduation and we can keep them on, especially a few who plan to go on to graduate school."

"Let me know if you need my help with the interviews. I have a few conference calls this afternoon then I'm heading out. Hit my cell if you need me."

Mike left the conference room curious and a little pissed that Loren had a date. He paused for a minute realizing this was definitely not him. He never cared that a woman he liked was seeing another guy, but this woman was Loren and he did care. He cared a lot. He went to his office wondering when Loren had met this guy and if she was seeing him before they slept together and if so, why didn't she tell him.

~~

Loren had experienced the week from hell at work. No matter how hard she tried, she was completely distracted with thoughts of Mike. She relived over and over again, the night they'd spent together. She knew that because she pushed back so hard on the idea of the two of them continuing to see each other, he had given her space to think things through.

Thoughts of their hot, sexy night together flooded her head daily. They had spoken a few times, but not about that night they spent in bed together. They kept the conversation about business and never talked personal, though she could tell that elephant was sitting high and pretty in the midst. To take her mind off of Mike and her desire for him, she was hoping to be able to relax tonight. She was going out to hear a new band at Jason's supper club and she wasn't going alone.

Weeks before her night with Mike, one of her sorority sisters had introduced her to a guy named Malcolm Waters and since she had not been able to return his phone call due to work, he had stopped by her office earlier in the week to introduce himself and invite her out to hear this new band that a friend of his was playing in. He was nice enough and she needed the distraction, so she agreed to go with him. They were meeting at the restaurant, that also happened to be the supper club, one of her favorite spots, since she didn't know what time she would be ready. Besides, just in case she wasn't having a good time, she could leave whenever she was ready. While she wrapped things up, she wondered what Mike was doing for the evening.

On more than one occasion she caught herself thinking about him with other women. She couldn't help it. She didn't mean to torture herself with the thought, but she knew how men were. She wondered if he thought about her as much as she thought about him. She needed to get back in the dating game. She couldn't see a way for things to work out between them and she wasn't going to spend all of her time pining away for him at home. Tonight she would go out and try to have a good time.

~~

Mike was glad to be done with work for the evening. His cell rang as he walked into his condo. Checking the display, he smiled when he saw it was Shelly; very predictable Shelly. It was Friday night and normally her phone call would mean an evening of wild sex. She had a thing for toys that many women found taboo, but not Shelly. She was open for just about anything he desired. Tonight, he wasn't having a desire for her. He had not desired her since before he slept with Loren. He answered her call because he knew if he didn't, she would continue to call and leave messages until he called her back.

"Hey Shelly."

"Hey handsome. What's up with you tonight? You feel like coming over and hanging out at my place? I found that deck of cards with all the sex positions that you love. I'm thinking tonight we could lay the cards face down and blindly select a few to experiment with. I've missed you and I have an itch that needs some major scratching and a fresh Brazilian wax that's calling your name."

She never ceased to amaze him. She never beat around the bush when it came to sex.

"As tempting as that sounds, I've had a long work day and I think I'm going to just chill. I actually brought some work home that I may delve into tonight to catch up."

"Wait, are you telling me you don't want to get into me, literally, tonight? I don't think you've ever turned me down before," she said, sounding confused.

"I know, but it's just work stuff. I told you with all the publicity my company has been getting over the past year, we've been swamped and until we hire the additional help around the office, we've all been working overtime to keep up with the new influx of projects. Can I get a rain check for another time?"

"Rain check? What the hell is that Mike? Rain check? What is that a code for you've found a new toy or what?"

"Shelly, that's not it at all. Like I said, it's just work." He was losing patience with her.

"Okay Mike, I hear you. Give me a call later if you change your mind or just drop by. Shop's always open for you."

He laughed. Her boldness was like so many women he dealt with. He needed to change the company he kept. Though he loved the acrobatic sex, he also realized he was getting to a place in his life where he needed women of more substance than a pair of big breasts and a penchant for doing whatever they could to please him sexually. In the back of their minds, he knew that if they could get him with sex, the rest of him would follow along. He wasn't looking for that.

"No problem Shelly. I'll give you a call."

He knew he wouldn't, but he needed to pacify her with a response that would buy him some time to figure out how to handle things with Loren. He hung up before Shelly could say anything more. For the first time in a long time, he questioned himself about the choices he'd been making when it came to women. He had been with a lot of women and had always practiced safe sex. By safe, he meant in more than just using condoms. He also meant safe in the type of women he dealt with.

It was important to him that he made it clear that he was only open to a friend with benefit type situation with any of them. He didn't want to be tied down and he didn't want them thinking of wedding dresses and kids because it wasn't him.

Walking through his condo, brought back memories of the night he'd spent with Loren. He didn't bring many women to his condo because he had dealt with his share of stalkers in the past and chose not to have every woman he bedded know where he laid his head. It made for a lot less drama. Tonight though, he couldn't imagine bringing any other women here again other than Loren. He didn't know what was going on with him, but that one night he and Loren spent together had sealed his fate. It had not been that long ago that she was here, in his bed, making love to his mind and his body like no woman ever had before. He had spent all the time since they were together honoring her wish of staying away from her, but the more he thought about it, the more he wasn't feeling that decision at all. He wasn't about to have a peaceful evening at home knowing she was out with someone.

Didn't Duron say Loren and her date were going to Jason's supper club tonight? He checked the time. It wasn't too late and he was quite hungry, not having eaten all day. Maybe he would just stop by the supper club and grab a bite to eat and at the same time, check out this guy Loren was out with tonight. He headed for the shower. He needed to see who this guy was that could make Loren want to go out with him after the incredible night they'd spent together.

Chapter 10

Loren and Malcolm's dinner had just arrived when Jason came over to the table to greet them.

"Loren, always good to see you," he said.

"Hey Jase."

Loren stood to give him a hug.

"Good to see you too."

She introduced him to her dinner date.

"Jason, this is Malcolm Waters. Malcolm this is Jason. He owns this supper club and is one of my brother's friends."

Jason and Malcolm shook hands.

"Feel free to call me Jase."

"Nice to meet you Jase," Malcolm said.

"I see business is jumping tonight. This place is packed and the band is awesome."

"Thanks Loren. Business has been booming. I'm actually looking into purchasing the building next door and expanding. With the crowds we've been seeing lately, it's definitely time. How's the family?"

"Everybody's great," Loren answered.

"That's good. Tell everyone hello. I'm going to let you

get back to your dinner. Enjoy."

"Thanks," Loren said as she retook her seat across from Malcolm.

When Jase walked back towards the kitchen, Loren turned her attention back to Malcolm.

"I didn't realize this place was black owned. Nice," Malcolm said. Loren could see he was impressed.

"Yes and he's doing really well. Your friend's band was great. Which one was he?"

"He was the drummer. We went to school together. They travel around a lot and I try to catch them whenever they come this way."

They continued to eat and enjoy idle chit chat. She was actually enjoying herself. He turned out to be the distraction she needed to take her mind off of work and off of Mike as well.

"I'm glad you agreed to finally go out with me Loren."

"I'm sorry for not getting back to you. I've been caught up with work and I've been traveling, so when Denise mentioned you to me and gave you my number, it's been hard trying to find time to return phone calls. I'm glad you stopped by my office and didn't give up on me. I'm not generally like that, but my business has really been picking up," Loren explained.

While they talked she'd learned a lot about him and was impressed with his line of work. He owned several fast food chains in the Atlanta area and was looking to expand to surrounding counties.

She lost her focus on what he was saying when she looked up and caught a glimpse of Mike at the bar. She wasn't sure it was him at first, until some people cleared out of the way and she was able to see him better. She nervously began nipping on her lip wondering what the odds were that he would show up on the night that she was here on a date. She didn't really want Mike to see her out, especially out with someone after she gave him her little speech about serial dating and here she was out with someone, not long after the night they were together.

Trying to conceal the view from him, she slid over a little bit so that Malcolm was blocking Mike's view of her. Maybe he wouldn't see her. She didn't know why she was reacting this way. She and Mike weren't dating. They were friends and she didn't need to hide when she was out on a date. Still she stayed out of his line of sight, hoping he was on a date as well. That thought made her feel a little down. She didn't really want to see him out with anyone.

For years it never bothered her to run into him with one woman or another out on a date. Now, the thought of it had her feeling sad, sick and jealous. It didn't occur to her how she would react, now that they had been intimate, to seeing him with someone else. She kept one ear on what Malcolm was saying and just smiled as he talked so that he couldn't see her distraction. She looked in Mike's direction again and to her it didn't appear that he was with anyone. There were several other gentlemen at the bar, but no women alone. That didn't mean he wasn't waiting on someone. She needed to stop torturing herself and focus on her date.

Mike looked up from his spot at the bar and noticed Jase was coming his way.

"Hey man," Jase said as he reached Mike.

"What's up bro?"

"Nothing but business twenty–four, seven. You waiting on a table? If you'd let me know you were coming I would have reserved one for you."

"No, I'm just going to grab some take-out."

Though Mike was talking to Jase, he continued looking around, trying to spot Loren.

Jase picked up on Mike's perusal of the crowd immediately and knew who he was looking for.

"Take-out, huh? Looking for someone in particular?"

Mike didn't answer. He just continued to look around.

"She's at the table in the far right corner Mike."

He tried to play it like he had no clue who Jase was talking about.

"Who? I'm not looking for anyone. I told you I'm just here to grab some take-out."

He knew Jase wasn't buying it.

Jason shook his head in disbelief that Mike was still playing the denial game.

"Mike, I told you this was not a good idea and to walk away. Obviously you didn't listen, so maybe you'd like to tell me what's going on here besides your obvious lie about showing up to get take-out?"

Mike looked in the direction of where Loren sat across from a man and anger started to rise up like he had never felt before. Not sure where the anger was coming from, he looked away and turned his attention back to Jase.

"Who is the guy Loren is with Jase? Do you know him? Have you seen him here before?"

"No, she did introduce us a while ago. All I know is his name is Malcolm. I only talked to her briefly. Why is something wrong?"

"Other than the fact that she's out with him? Not that I know of," Mike answered with disgust in his voice.

"Duron didn't know who she was going out with tonight

and he was a little concerned. You know the incident with the last serious relationship Loren had that almost landed Duron in jail. He's just protective I guess. He mentioned she would be here and I thought I would check this guy out for him."

"Sure you did. Your being here is all about looking out for Loren on behalf of her brother who wants to protect her from the big bad wolves of the world. It has nothing to do with the fact that you have a thing for her yourself? Come on Mike, it's me."

He hesitated then decided to come clean.

"Okay, so yeah I have a thing for her. It's an unexpected thing. It's hitting me over and over like a ton of bricks."

Mike turned his attention back to Loren. When he did, he noticed that she was looking right at him. He continued to stare at her no matter how hard she tried to not look at him and focus on her date. He wasn't going to make it easy for her. He sat back on his stool, ordered a beer and just waited, never taking his eyes off of her.

Jase could see that his friend was not happy seeing Loren out on a date and it had nothing to do with looking out for her for Duron. He was looking out for her for him.

"Don't do it Mike. I told you before, walk away man. I'm looking at the two of you looking at each other and it's a good thing I have a sprinkler system because you two could start a fire up in here."

Mike knew he was right, but he was past walking away. It was already too late for him.

"Jase, I hear you. Too late buddy."

"Mike, tell me you didn't?"

Mike turned and looked at him clueless.

"Didn't what?"

"Tell me you did not sleep with Loren."

There was no avoiding the obvious with his friend so he avoided answering and turned back to look at Loren and her date.

"Mike?"

He knew his friend wasn't going to let up.

"No can do bruh. I did and now she's out on a date with some other guy. It's taking every ounce of energy I have to keep from going over there and knocking his ass out."

"Mike, man why don't you go up in my office and cool off. This is not a good look for you."

"No I'm good. I won't make a scene. I just wanted to see for myself if she was really out with someone tonight and I got my answer. I'm going to order some food and head home. Can you get me my usual?" Mike asked.

"Yeah I will, but Mike, listen to me. Don't go over there. Nothing good will come out of that. Don't move from this stool. The guy has no idea you slept with Loren and he has no clue who you are so don't make a scene. Just sit tight and I'll get your order placed."

"Jase, man I'm not trying to start any trouble up in your spot. I'm cool right here."

Loren could feel the penetrating stare Mike was giving her. He had seen her and her date and if Loren was correct, he was angry about it. His expression never changed. He stared at her giving her a look as if he were asking her what the hell she was doing out with this guy. As much as Loren wanted to ignore Mike's presence, she knew it wasn't going to happen. She decided to go over and say hello. She excused herself from the table. There was no need to continue the staring match when clearly there were words that needed to be said.

Mike saw her get up from the table and head in his direction and he was prepared. He had a few questions to ask her. When she approached, he let her speak first.

"Hi, Mike. What are you doing here? Are you here with someone?" she asked.

Mike tampered down his anger at her being out on a date with someone only days after being in bed with him.

"I'm here grabbing take-out and no I'm not here with anyone. I see you can't say the same thing," he said, not trying to hide his displeasure.

Loren didn't immediately respond as she looked from Mike, over to the table where her date still sat waiting for her and then back to Mike again. All she could think about was how good Mike looked. Even in a simple button down shirt and jeans he looked scrumptious. She was so busy gawking at him, she didn't realize he was waiting for some type of reply from her. She didn't hear what he may have said so she didn't know what she should be responding to.

Mike could feel his temper rising and knew he needed to control it. He and Loren had sex. They were not involved so he had no right to be as angry as he was. He softened the conversation.

"You look nice Loren," he said, breaking into the silent moment.

Loren checked back into the conversation.

"Thank you. You look nice yourself."

"I hope you're having a nice time on your date," he sneered.

She could hear the distain in his statement. She played along, but ignored what appeared to be a little tension between them, definitely a result of her being out on a date.

"I am thank you. He's a nice guy."

"Who is he?"

"I met him through one of my sorority sisters weeks ago. She thought we would hit it off."

Loren wanted to be sure to stress that she did not just meet Malcolm.

"We have been trying to connect since then and our schedules didn't seem to match up until recently."

Mike didn't say anything immediately. He didn't want to talk about his guy with her.

"Loren, I don't care about this dude or when you met him. What I do care about is you and why you're out with him."

"I told you, he asked me out. He has a friend that played in the band and he asked if I would have dinner and check the band out and I said yes."

Mike was looking at her as if he could see right through her.

"So this is it Loren? I think we have a lot to talk about, but apparently you don't think so. Is this your answer to our situation? Is this your way of letting me know that I need to be satisfied with the one night we spent together and not think about taking things further? After all you did give me the speech about you wanting a monogamous relationship so I'm assuming this guy is the start of your search for that? No consideration of being with me at all? Was I your version of your stint with casual sex and now you can find someone else to get serious with?"

She could see that this was not the time or place to have this conversation with him.

"Mike, can we talk about this another time, please?"

"When Loren? Should I save this for talk on the plane out to California? What, you'll call me in the morning after your date tonight?" he snorted out.

Loren wasn't pleased with how he stressed the word after. He sounded like he was implying something would be happening between her and Malcolm.

Loren chose her words carefully.

"I need to get back to my date. I'll call you tomorrow."

They were staring at each other, neither making a move. When he didn't give any type of response, she turned to walk back to her table. Before she could get away, Mike grabbed her hand and pulled her back so that her ear was close to his lips.

"So I'm not supposed to want you again after the night we spent together? Should I just forget about it like you obviously have?"

He was hurt and Loren didn't want that. She also needed him to know that the night with him was everything to her.

"Is that what you think? That I've forgotten about the best night of my life spent with you? It's all I've been able to think about. What am I supposed to do here? I can't just walk around in a state of constant heat all of the time, every single time we see each other. Neither one of us would survive. I'm ashamed at the thoughts I'm having right now because I know it's wrong. I am out on a date with someone and at this moment I'm remembering what you tasted like."

When Loren said those words she looked him right in the eye.

"I know we agreed to stay away from each other, but that hasn't kept me from thinking about it."

"Loren, you made the decision that we should stay away from each other. That wasn't a mutual decision, nor did I agree, if you remember."

"So what, are you telling me, you haven't been seeing anyone? You haven't been with anyone? Magic Stick Mike is giving up casual women?" she scoffed.

Mike looked at her in total shock that she used the name he'd heard some of the women he'd had sex with used to describe him. He was too shocked to even respond. He used to think the term was funny when he heard other women say it, but coming from Loren it sounded demeaning and he hated it.

"What? You think I didn't know what the women call you? I swear, I don't know why you and my brother think I don't know about all the women you have made your way through. Don't be shocked because I'm out on a date tonight. I can't just sit at home and wonder who you are bedding and wallow in self-pity knowing that I would love for it to be me."

Now Mike was bothered that apparently Loren was feeling hurt that they aren't together and that it's not just him feeling that way.

"It could be you Loren. All you have to do is give us a chance. I have not been with anyone and have not been able to stop thinking about you since the night we spent together, so yeah, the last thing I'm thinking about is having anyone in my bed, but you."

All she could think about was how his lips moved when he spoke. She was thinking of the incredible things that mouth did to her. The many ways those lips pleasured her. She needed to get away from him and back to her date. She needed to put some distance between them. Just as she started to move away, Mike reached out to grab her hand and pull her back to him again. He wasn't going to tempt her anymore. He would do the gentlemanly thing and let her get back to her date in peace.

"I hope you enjoy the rest of your date Loren."

That was all Mike said before releasing her hand and running his finger from the inside of her elbow down to her wrist. She was taken aback by her sudden want for him just from that one gesture. He remembered that the fleshy part of her arm was a spot that turned her on. Her breath caught when she looked up into the deep chocolate brown eyes that were hooded with yearning for her. She felt ready to explode on the spot. Unable to bear any more, she turned and walked back to her table on wobbly legs. Legs that she felt sure would give out on her before she reached her destination.

After re-taking her seat, Loren couldn't concentrate on anything after her encounter with Mike. Malcolm was talking, but she heard nothing. Music was playing, but it didn't interest her. She hadn't finished her food, but she no longer had an appetite. No matter how she tried to focus on being present at the table, she couldn't help but look beyond her table into the intense stare coming from Mike at the bar. He had not left yet. He was still sitting there, never taking his eyes off of her. She wondered if he had any idea what his look was doing to her. She wanted him badly. More than she did the night in his condo. She needed to look away, but couldn't.

As Malcolm was talking, whenever he looked down or away from her face, she looked at Mike, only to find him giving her the sexiest look. He was definitely playing dirty tonight and he knew it. Loren thought she even saw him smile one time when he noticed how uncomfortable his presence was making her. All he had to do was give her one look and her body longed for him. What was wrong with her? She was sitting here with one man who was very nice and charming and all she could think about was taking a ride on the magic stick that is Mike. She picked up her glass of water to try and cool down. Her date looked at her and took that as maybe she wasn't feeling too well.

"Loren, are you alright? You look a little flustered? Are you feeling okay?"

"I'm feeling fine. I think it's just been a long work week. I should probably head home."

"No problem. Let me run to the men's room and I'll walk you out to your car."

Loren nodded. Her mouth was dry from watching Mike across the room. He never stopped looking at her the whole time. He looked at her as if he too were reminiscing about the night they spent together. If his thoughts were anything like hers, he was remembering the feel of them touching skin to skin in the most intimate way. She was remembering the fiery kisses they shared and the look in his eyes said he was remembering the same thing. Loren was so aroused from the combination of her memories and his gaze at her. She wanted him again and she had since the moment she left him, the morning after the night they spent together. That need hadn't lessened and right now, it was reaching a peak.

When Malcolm got up to go to the men's room, Loren focused all of her attention back on Mike. He wasn't eating or drinking. He was looking at her and she wished he would stop. It was as if he were trying to send her a message using only his eyes. As wrong as she knew she was since she was on a date with another man, she was trying to send him a message as well. Her message was she needed and wanted him bad. She didn't care who she was on a date with. She wanted to rip every stitch of clothing off of his body and take every delight he could offer her and if the night they were together was any sign, he had plenty to offer.

Loren broke the connection between the two of them long enough to reach for her purse to find her cell phone. She was beyond walking away from the inevitable. She took it out, searched her contacts for Mike's cell and typed out a one line text message to him. The message read, *'my place in an hour.'* After typing her message, she looked back over at Mike, held up her phone to signal to him that she'd sent him a message. She watched him reached for his cell. She held on to her cell phone, waiting to see if he would respond. What she saw was Mike read her message, place his phone back in ith s holster on his hip and gulp down the last of his beer. He stood from the stool, look quickly at her, turned and headed for the door. She sat nervously wondering why he didn't reply to her text. She kept checking it and didn't realize Malcolm was back. She jumped when he spoke, surprised by his reappearance.

"Are you ready to go?"

"Yes."

She watched as he came around to pull out her chair.

"I had a wonderful time with you tonight Loren. I hope I can see you again."

"Thank you. I had a wonderful time as well. Sure we can go out again. I look forward to it. Deep down, she really didn't."

Chapter 11

Mike sat in his car outside Loren's condo waiting for her to get home. He knew he should have replied to her text with either a yes or a no or any type of response, but he decided against it. He wanted his actions to speak louder than any words he could have texted back to her. Since he was parked on the front side of the condo, he was able to see when the light in her place went on. He figured she would enter her building through the garage which was safer because there were guards who would be sure she made it to her door safely. When he saw her light go on, he got out of his car and headed toward the building. As soon as he rang her bell, she answered right away.

"It's Mike, Loren."

He heard the buzzer which released the door latch.

When he reached her front door, he was about to knock when the door opened. On the other side of the door stood the most beautiful site. Loren was still dressed in the dress she wore on her date. Seeing her, he wanted her and his plan was to take it off of her immediately. He didn't want to stand in the hall of her condo and devour her so he entered and waited until she locked the door behind him.

When she turned back to him, neither one of them said a word.

Loren tried to outstare Mike, but it wasn't working. She had to look away to keep her head clean of all of the naughty thoughts about him she had been having since she'd seen him at the restaurant.

"Look at me Loren."

She continued to look away.

Dropping his voice an octave, he repeated himself.

"Loren, look at me."

When she did, she was shocked at the depth of thirst she saw in his eyes.

"You summoned for me and I'm here Loren. What are you going to do with me?"

Loren gulped, trying to find the words to say something, anything.

She watched in what seemed like slow motion, as Mike lifted his hand and with one finger, he ran it across her neck making her skin tingle.

"Loren, what were you thinking before I got here?"

She wasn't sure she heard him. That one single finger that was stroking her neck was gliding first around her neck and then he would use it to dip down the center of the top of her dress and then back up to her neck, teasing her. She was unable to think clearly.

"What?"

"I said, what were you thinking before I got here?"

She wasn't sure if she should tell him the truth. She bet nothing shocked or surprised him, but she wasn't sure she wanted to share her most intimate thoughts about him. Ever since she spotted him at the restaurant, she couldn't get visions of the two of them from the night they'd spent together and the many looks on his face as he stroked in and out of her body. She began remembering the seductive words he'd whisper of all of the things he wanted to do to her, right before he did them. Even now, standing in her living room, she was imagining them rolling around in her bed fighting with him over who would be on top.

She already knew what she wanted him to do to her and invading her thoughts were ideas of all of the things she wanted to do to him.

It was a good thing he showed up. She would have had to seek her own personal release if he hadn't, in order to find any rest. She was already set with the toy she was going to use in place of him if he had not shown up. It was those thoughts that were going through her mind when he rang her bell. She wasn't sure she could tell him that she was thinking about doing all sorts of nasty things to pleasure herself if he had not shown up. She trembled at the thought of telling him all about that.

When she went to look away again, Mike reached out softly and turned her face back to him. He caressed her cheek softly and then replaced the finger on her cheek with his lips, kissing her softly. He then whispered in her ear.

"I know it had to be something very naughty because I can read it on your face. Tell me, was it about me?"

Loren didn't dare speak, afraid of what may come out of her mouth so she nodded her head.

"Were you thinking of the night we spent together where I tasted every single spot on your luscious body? Or were you thinking of how you returned the favor and made love to my body with your mouth?"

Loren trembled at his words and he felt it.

"I see I'm hitting a spot. Something else I'm going to

discover tonight, perhaps is that you like to hear me talk that way to you."

She wasn't sure she was going to be able to take anymore.

He continued kissing her on the side of her face getting closer and closer to her ear.

"Are you going to tell me what you were thinking or do I need to continue to guess?"

Nibbling feverishly on her lips, she whispered her response very softly, feeling a little bit ashamed and a whole lot turned on.

"I was wondering if you were going to show up or not."

Mike was intrigued. Surely that thought alone wasn't what had put such a flushed looked on her face when she opened the door. He edged her on further by licking around her ear lobe, a spot he knew would drive her crazy with want.

"Why would I not come tonight? You sent me a text message and as much as you know I want to be with you, you had a doubt I wouldn't be here, now? I want you to know I would meet you anywhere, anytime. I don't care who you go out on dates with. I know the connection we share and I don't care how much you want to deny it, you're going to remember me and think about me, just as I do with you. I'm going to be in the back of your mind. I will admit I was disappointed to see you with someone else tonight. Call it jealousy if you want, I don't care. All I know is if you're trying to erase thoughts of being with me by going out with someone else, it won't work. This, between us, is inevitable and you need to remember that. So, what else?"

Loren had to clear her throat she was so sated with

need.

"I was thinking about what I would do if you didn't come."

Loren knew it was too late. The thoughts had turned to words and were out of her mouth. She kept doing that. She could look at Mike and see that he knew were her thoughts were going.

"Oh, so are you saying you didn't know if I would come over or you didn't know if I would come? You know they aren't the same thing right?"

The room was getting very hot, she thought. Maybe she needed to turn on her air conditioning.

Mike was playing very dirty with her, but he couldn't resist. He was not happy seeing her with someone else tonight and he was going to make sure that by the time he left her condo, there would be no doubt about the direction they would be headed and she would know that he had no plans of going along with her plan of them staying away from each other. He would not accept her going out with anyone that wasn't him.

While in his thoughts, he realized Loren hadn't answered him.

"Loren?"

Before he could ask her again she responded, "Both."

"Interesting," he murmured in her ear.

He decided to increase the pressure and the temperature by moving his lips away from her face and down the side of her neck, continuing to tantalize her with words and kisses.

"Just what were your plans if I had not come over?"

The fact that he dropped his voice and whispered his words while his tongue did unimaginable things to her was teasing on a level Loren had never experienced before. Her body was burning up. She tried to concentrate on answering and he was making it harder and harder to do so.

"Things," she whispered back.

"Things, Loren? By things do you mean toy things?"

Loren shook her head, happy that she didn't have to say it.

Mike grinned against her ear at the image that formed in his head of Loren pleasuring herself while thinking about him.

"Baby, never be shy around me. I want to know what you like so that I'll know how to please you. Right now, we'll table the toy discussion for later. I have other plans that are of a more immediate concern."

Loren didn't know what to say. She wanted him with a wildness that she had never experienced before. Her thong was drenched, she had sweat forming in the most intimate places and all this dirty talk was wreaking havoc on her senses.

Mike turned her face up to look directly at him and as he leaned down towards her, she lifted slightly up towards him rising on the tips of her toes as he planted a killer kiss filled with the promise of everything he had planned for them for the night and she was more than ready to receive it all. She just needed him to stop torturing her and do something about the ache in between her legs.

After the first touch of her lips to his, she watched as he snaked his tongue out to lick across the seam of her lips. Before she knew what was happening, she grasped his tongue between her teeth and sucked it into her mouth as if she were suffering from starvation. What started out as a soft, sensual kiss, quickly turned into a duel of the tongues. They were like two starving, crazed maniacs who could not get enough of each other.

Mike's desire to be inside of Loren had him dispensing with any more discussion or pleasantries. He reached down for the hem of her dress. He didn't remove it just yet. He never lost eye contact as he slid his hands up the outside of her thighs, all the way up her legs until he came in contact with the edge of her panties. He slid them down, not softly or even slowly. He dragged them down like a man on a mission. Once he had them all the way down, he watched as Loren lifted her feet so that he could take them completely off. When he had them clear, he ran the crotch across his nose, loving the scent of her on them. That act had Loren on the precipice of exploding. Her body was beyond ready and she was more than excited and had no problem with begging.

"No more nicety Mike. Take me please."

Mike heard the need in her voice. He recognized it because it matched his own. He didn't say a word. He didn't want to ruin the moment with conversation. He reached into his back pocket, withdrew a condom from his wallet, tossed the wallet, unzipped his pants, pulled out his more than ready, erect, and hard as steel flesh and covered it with the condom. He felt like a teenager fumbling around because his need to be inside of her was so great.

He couldn't seem to get inside of her fast enough. Time seemed to be moving in slow motion and it appeared both of them were inpatient tonight.

Finally getting the condom in place, he wasted no time moving them to the nearest chair. He moved so that Loren sat back on the chair. He knelt down in between her legs, pulled her by her legs until her buttocks were at the very edge. He spread her legs, and planted himself in her as far as he could go, every glorious inch by glorious inch until all ten were deeply entrenched. The sudden invasion caused them both to gasp at the same time, loving the pleasure of the action.

"Oh baby, this is even better than the first time," Mike crooned in her ear.

She leaned up a little, close to his ears and said, "I don't want nice, slow, seductive Mike tonight. I want you to give it to me hard and fast, please," she begged.

He looked at her before planting a hard and demanding kiss on her lips.

"I told you the first time we were together, I aim to please; however you want it, so hold on sweetheart, this ride is going to be bumpy."

Mike started pumping into her so hard the chair started moving backwards closer to the wall. Loren did as he said and held on tight and enjoyed the ride. She could tell she was about to get the ride of her life. Each thrust into her body had them grunting on each and every plunge. He was riding her like a stallion and she threw that stallion like action right back at him. She needed this. She needed him. It was obvious he needed this as well. They were going along at a steady, hard, but fast pace just like Loren wanted. Mike's thrusts into her body matched the one's his tongue was making in her mouth. This time with Mike was epic. Her body was on cloud nine and she felt like she couldn't get enough of him. She was flying, soaring to the highest heights as her orgasm slammed into her faster than expected, but very much wanted and needed. Not long after her own eruption, she felt Mike stiffen as he too climaxed and let go.

Loren lay in Mike's arms on her living room sofa. They never made it to the bedroom. She hoped he didn't have plans to get up and head to the bedroom unless he planned on carrying her. She didn't think she had the strength to get up and walk on her own. Her body had just received a workout that could equal a few hours at the gym.

"Loren, baby, are you awake?"

Loren definitely wasn't asleep. How could she sleep being this close to him? All she could think about was how good it felt to be wrapped in his arms so tightly again. Hearing his heart beat against her ear was soothing and she could lay like this all night. She lifted her head so that she could look directly into his eyes; eyes that she was becoming addicted to looking into.

"Yes, but just barely," she was finally able to say.

Mike laughed at her.

"I thought for sure you would be knocked out. I know you wore me out. If it wasn't for the fact that I don't quite fit comfortably on your sofa, I would be out like a light myself."

"Well my sofa is regular length, so it's not my fault that at six foot three, half of your body is hanging over the side," she laughed.

"Yeah, well I would have gotten up and moved us to the bed by now, but you gave a brother more than a workout."

Loren slid a little further up his body so that they were cheek to cheek. She loved the feel of his scruffy beard on her skin.

"Your body isn't the only one feeling like it had a workout. I'm aching in places I didn't realize I could ache."

Mike leaned over and gave Loren a soft kiss on the

cheek.

"I'm sorry. I didn't mean to take you so rough, but I couldn't contain myself. You really bring out the animal in me. You are so responsive to me, each time I tried to pull it back some, to not hurt you, you pulled more out of me. I didn't mean to lose control like I did."

Mike I asked for it, remember? I know you feel the need to be gentle and caring with me, but it's okay to lose control. I love it when you let lose."

She tingled when he began rubbing up and down her spine with the pad of his fingers. Though her body ached in a very good way, it started to stir again with a deep longing.

"We need to get off of this sofa. It's not good for either of us; well unless I'm inside of you then all bets of being uncomfortable are off," Mike added.

He moved to get them both off of the sofa when he heard Loren gasp.

"Are you sore Loren?"

"A little, but in a very nice, I have just been thoroughly sexed, kind of way."

Mike moved to get up and slide Loren on to the sofa. He could hear her moan of protest when he separated them.

"I'll be right back sweetheart," Mike said as he slid from under her and headed in the direction of her bathroom. He first needed to discard the condom that had seen better days and to also run a nice hot bath so that he could help ease some of the discomfort he had caused. He knew she had to be sore. He had been completely out of control during their love making, but the more he tried to hold back on how aggressive he knew he could be sexually, he couldn't because of how badly he wanted her.

When he returned to the living room, Loren had nodded off. He leaned down to gather her up in his arms.

"Loren, baby, wake up. Let's get you off of this sofa and in a tub of hot water. Without it, you are going to be very sore by the time you wake in the morning."

He reached to lift her up as she wrapped her arms around his neck.

"I don't want to lose all of the feeling of what we just did. I want to walk around all day tomorrow with the lovely aches from tonight."

"You say that now sweetness, but you'll be singing a different tune in the morning."

He took Loren into the bathroom to let her soak while he figured out what the next step would be for them. He wasn't going to lose her. He just had to make her see that things with them could work out. They just needed time to be together and see how good they could be.

Chapter 12

In the morning, Loren woke with her back up against what felt like a solid wall. She looked over to see that Mike was still asleep. She didn't want to wake him. She gently turned over and looked at his handsome face as he slept.

"What happens now Loren?" Mike asked with his eyes still closed. He could feel her when she woke up and turned towards him.

His speaking caught her off guard, considering she thought he was still asleep.

"Tell me so that I'll know if I'm supposed to continue to act like we didn't just have another marathon night of incredible sex. I also don't want you to think this is just about the sex because it isn't. I've been reserved for a long time holding my feelings for you in check and I don't want to have to do that anymore, but I also know it's not my call, it's yours."

Loren had been thinking the same thing before she moved around after waking. She knew how he felt because she felt the same way, but again in the light of day, the obvious was clear; there was no way she could think of to make this work without all hell breaking loose in their lives.

"What do you want me to say here?" she asked.

Mike wasn't ready to hear her try to convince him again that they wouldn't work. He turned so that he was facing the opposite direction. He didn't want her to see the anger he knew his face would show.

"Mike, turn back around please."

Instead of turning around, he sat up.

"You know what I want you to say Loren? I want you to say that you want to be with me as much as I want to be with you. I want you to say that you don't give a damn what anyone else thinks about our being together. Are you ready to say that or are you going to tell me again about how this was a mistake and we can't do this again? Are you going to say my friendship and partnership with your brother could be ruined if he found out about us? That's beginning to sound like a broken record."

When she didn't answer, he knew he had his answer. He got up to leave the room, knowing they were about to have an argument.

Loren hollered after him.

"Can you come back in the room please and talk to me instead of making a dash for the door in anger? Don't leave like this," she pleaded.

Mike turned around, came back into the room and walked right over to her and waited. He'd said what he needed to say, but he wanted to give her the chance to have more of a say too.

"Mike, do you know I know you just as well as I know my own brothers? I have spent as much time around you over the years as I have with them. Just as I believe I know you very well, you know me also. Let me tell you what I know about you. For starters, I know you love women. Not just a woman in particular, but you love women. I know it, you know it, my brother knows it and yes I believe it could be a problem. I have dealt with my share of players and I won't willingly get involved with one. I made a promise to myself that I would only get involved with someone when I knew it could lead to something serious. I would like nothing more than to be with you, but could you really say you would be willing to give up the random women you so love bedding on a regular basis to be involved with me and only me? Are you really ready to convince my brother when he finds out, that you aren't playing me to temporarily ease an itch you want to scratch? Remember, he knows you too."

Mike wasn't giving up.

"So, what are we supposed to do, just go about our lives like we aren't falling for each other? I don't know about you Loren, but I can't stop thinking about you. I'm not thinking about any other women. I'm thinking only about you. What will you do? Try to make a relationship work with this Malcolm dude you were out with last night? Let's keep in mind all the pretending we'll both have to do acting as if we don't feel the chemistry between us that I believe is far beyond just the great sex we've had. I think we owe it to each other to see where this could go."

Loren didn't want to walk away from him either. How could they make this work, she thought.

"What would we do Mike? Sneak around like a couple of teenagers? Suppose this doesn't work out between you and me? If everyone knows about us and it doesn't work out or if it ends badly, what then? Think of what it could do to your business relationship, not to mention the personal relationship with my brother, with my family. I know I keep bringing that up, but you guys have built something incredible in the business world. I couldn't forgive myself if it were negatively impacted because of me."

Enough of this, he thought.

"Why don't we see how things would pan out before we tell anyone? I'm willing to keep it from everyone while we take the time to get to know each other beyond the connection we have had all these years. Do you know I have never had a serious relationship with a woman before? Of course through the college years it was all about getting some and getting plenty and along with your brother and Tyrone, we did that. After graduate school, we started the business and I have given all of my attention to that. When I realized I had a thing for you, things really started to change for me. Jase recognized it too and pulled me up about it, twice. I will admit, I have not been a saint when it comes to the ladies, but I'm willing to give up being with any other woman if it meant you would give us an honest chance. I mean a real chance Loren."

Mike saw the mystified look on Loren's face and wasn't sure what part of his statement caused the look of wonder.

"Wait, Jase pulled you up again? You never did go into detail when you told me he said something to you before."

Mike knew it was time to lay it all out for her.

"That night we had dinner to talk about the house, he cornered me in his office and told me he saw the way I was looking at you and dancing with you and he told me I was treading in dangerous territory because he knew Duron would not like it. I brushed him off, but he mentioned it again last night when he saw me at the restaurant. He knows about us, but I know he would never say anything so don't worry."

Loren sat up in the bed while Mike sat in the lounge chair across from her. He leaned forward and looked her straight in the eyes. He wanted to be sure he was completely honest with her about everything about himself and he needed to start with telling her how he ended up at the restaurant the night before."

"Duron told me you would be at the restaurant last night. That's why I was there. I wanted to see this guy you were going to be out with. We were talking in his office earlier in the day and he mentioned you were originally supposed to have plans with Taija, but you broke them because you had a date. I admit I was angry, but I didn't let it show. It pissed me off that you seemed to dismiss what we shared so easily and go out with some dude that according to your brother, no one knew anything about. My mind played tricks on me and I came to see you and to see who you were with."

She knew his presence at the supper club was no coincidence, but she didn't want to assume anything. Knowing how her night turned out, she didn't mind and if she were honest with herself, she'd admit she was happy to see him when he showed up. For now, they needed to resolve this before he left.

"Mike, are you really willing to sneak around with me until I'm convinced we really have something worth sharing with family and friends? It would also mean you can't casually date other women. I couldn't handle the thought of you being with anyone else, but me. Before you respond, I know that sounds selfish, but I'm being honest here. I don't like to share and if we're going to do this, there can't be any distractions of other women."

"Baby, I have no problem with that. After the workout you gave a brother tonight, I'm not sure I'd even have the energy to entertain anyone else, nor would I want to. You also have to agree, no more dates with Malcolm or anyone else. If having you means you need some time before we tell anyone about us, I'm willing to go along with that because you're worth it."

A smile crept on Loren's face as she scooted out of bed, moved closer to him and leaned into those lips she was slowly becoming hooked on tasting.

"Shall we seal this with a kiss?" she asked.

At this point, Mike knew he would give her anything she asked for. She just gave him the one thing he wanted; her.

"You can have anything you want," he said moving closer so that he could capture her lips and fill it the moment with a promise.

Chapter 13

A few weeks had passed since she and Mike had agreed on a secret relationship and Loren was happier than she ever remembered being in her life. So far, they had been able to keep their affair a secret from everyone. She didn't want to broadcast that they were seeing each other, even though he constantly pressured her to do so. They spent many nights at her condo so that they wouldn't run in to anyone at his, knowing he shared the penthouse level space of his condo with Duron and Tyrone.

They weren't able to date out in the open in the Atlanta area, but they were able to do lots of dating on their business trips to California. She spent hours during the day working on Mike's house while he worked at the new office taking care of business. They spent evenings out at dinner, taking in shows or movies and one evening, they even went to Disneyland.

Now back in Atlanta from her latest west coast trip, she was enjoying a day of shopping and had plans to visit her parents and then meet Taija for lunch and find out what was going on with her and Duron. Apparently while she was so focused on her happiness, she didn't realize the relationship between her brother Duron and Taija had fizzled. She would find out more about that while talking to Taija later.

"Hey mom," Loren said as she exited her car and saw her mom working in her garden after pulling into the driveway at her parents' house.

"Hey baby girl. It's good to see my only daughter."

Loren felt bad. She figured her parents were busy preparing for the gala that was coming up soon and that they wouldn't notice she had not been around as often as she normally would be.

"I'm sorry mom. With work picking up, I've been crazy busy. How are plans for the hospital gala coming along?"

Loren knew that the hospital where her father served as chief of surgery had an annual fundraiser and she looked forward to going every year. She was happy that she convinced Mike to go even if they couldn't go as a couple. They would at least get to spend the evening around each other.

"The plans are on target," her mother said.

"Your father says that it looks like all of the tickets were sold this year as well. The money this will raise for the free clinic will help keep it operating in the black. It's good to know that in this crazy world we are living in now, people still have a soft heart for each other."

"You are right about that mom. Listen, have you heard from Duron? I hear there are some issues with him and Taija."

"All I know is that he had done some work at the cabin last week and whatever was bothering him, he doesn't want to talk about it. I assume when he's ready, he'll let us know what's going on. For now, I'm letting him have his space."

"I invited Taija to come with us when we go shopping for our gowns for the gala. She said she wasn't going to go, but I'm hoping she will change her mind."

"I'm sure she's a little hesitant with the current problems she and Duron are having. If she wants to go, there will be a ticket for her no matter what."

"Thanks mom. I'm going to go sit and talk with dad for a bit."

"Okay. He was just saying he wondered what was going on with his wayward daughter. He was going to send the forces out to look for you."

"I know and again I'm sorry for not making the time to stop by. I have been calling everyday so that should give me some credit."

She smiled when her mother smiled letting her know all was well.

"I know and I told him you've been doing a lot of travel working on Mike's house in California. How is that coming along?"

For a second, Loren's mind wandered to the hot, lust-filled nights she'd spent with Mike, but quickly dispensed those thoughts knowing she couldn't let on that things between she and Mike were more than just a friendly business arrangement.

"It's coming along fine. His house is beautiful and he's loved all of the ideas I've had for the space."

"I'm going to miss having him around all the time when he finally moves. He's like a son and I love having him over for dinner, attacking his meals like he never gets a homemade meal."

Loren's smile withered as she thought about the possibility of Mike actually moving. She'd been so busy living in the moment and enjoying her time with him that she hadn't had time to think about what would happen when his time in Atlanta would be up. What would they do about their relationship? She knew they needed to talk about it.

"I know he thinks of you as a second mom and will miss being around too, but I'm sure he'll make many trips back to Atlanta. This is still his home."

"That's true, but I'm hoping, just as I do with my own children that he'll settle down soon with a wife and some babies and then he'll have less time to spend traveling back and forth."

Loren watched her mother work in her garden and dismissed any thoughts of Mike marrying someone let alone, having babies with anyone that wasn't her. The thought that he could do that made her tremble and not in the sexy, hot way she did when she thought about him. She trembled knowing that it could be a possibility if things didn't work out for them. She shook off all thoughts of him with anyone other than her and headed toward the door to spend some time with her dad.

At her back her mother smiled knowing she'd hit a nerve with her remark about Mike getting married and having children with someone. Her kids thought they were able to hide things from her, but just as with her other children, she knew everything about her daughter. For now, she would keep quiet about her suspicions regarding Loren's true feelings for Mike. She would let Loren come to her. For now, she smiled knowing that one day, she hoped Mike would be more of a son than he already was. She knew Loren was thinking about the idea of Mike with someone else that wasn't her and she also knew from

Loren's silence that the idea of that, wasn't sitting well.

~~

Mike was happy and everyone around him noticed the change in him. It's not that he wasn't a happy type of guy to begin with, but he had to admit even to himself that his happiness was over the top since he and Loren had been seeing each other and had somehow been able to keep it from everyone. They were learning more and more about each other and when he was away from her, he thought about her constantly.

He was currently in his office making plans to take a final flight out to California before the final move which was scheduled to take place in about three months. His cell phone rang interrupting his thoughts. He looked at the display and noticed it was Shelly calling again. He had not seen her in weeks and she was getting persistent about seeing him. He had spoken to her a few times to let her know that they would not be seeing each other anymore. She apparently didn't take the conversation too serious because she continued to call him and allude to them hooking up, something he no longer had any interest in with her.

He didn't know what else he needed to say to get her to understand that things were over between the two of them. They weren't involved in any type of relationship; they had been sex buddies for a few years and on occasions when he needed to scratch an itch, like she did, they would hook up without any notions of commitment. She was a beautiful woman, but he was no longer interested. Lately, her calls had been much more frequent and she was becoming agitated that he didn't want to see her anymore. He tried to explain to her that he was in a committed relationship and did not spend time with other women anymore, including her. Rather than have another conversation with her that would lead nowhere, he decided to ignore her all together. He hoped she'd get the point and stop contacting him.

There was something strange about Shelly that he couldn't quite put his finger on and it had to do with odd sightings of her while he was out and about. He thought he'd seen her a few times when he and Loren were able to sneak in a late night movie or have dinner at an out of the way restaurant. If he didn't know any better he would think that she was stalking him. He figured that soon she'd realize that he was serious about Loren and had no plans to go back to his old ways of hooking up with women for pleasure. Loren was all he needed.

Thinking of Loren had him smiling again and his thoughts turned to a Saturday afternoon they recently spent indoors all day. He seldom had Saturdays where he could do nothing. Loren with her interior design business never had Saturdays off, but with the new help she had hired, she was able to make more free time for herself and for them.

On this particular Saturday, he was finally able to get a look at Loren's sex toy collection that she kept hidden in her bedroom. He took great pleasure in how sexually liberated Loren was becoming around him. Nothing was off limits between them and she had no problem expressing to him what pleased her. He loved introducing several of the toys in her collection into their sex life. He believed just like in business, you have to constantly reinvent your sex life as well in order to keep it fresh. That was something they certainly did.

Thinking back on that day, he now felt the urge to see her. He reached for his cell to call her when his assistant told him he had several messages from Shelly. Now that he'd been ignoring her calls to his cell phone, it now appears that she was calling him at the office, something she never did and something he had no plans of tolerating. He was going to have to have a face to face conversation with her so that he could be sure she understood things were completely over between them. That would have to wait because right now, his mind was only on Loren. He thanked his assistant and when she walked out of his office, he tossed the messages in the trash. He didn't want to think of anything, but Loren so he called her to see if they could have a movie night. Since dating him, she had gotten over her fear of scary movies, especially after watching them, he was always there with her in the night if she had a nightmare.

He called her cell phone and when she didn't answer, he called her office, something he seldom did especially since they were still keeping things pretty quiet.

"LKnight Designs, this is Bria, how may I help you?"

"Hello, this is Michael Bailey calling for Ms. Knight. Is she available?"

"Hold please."

Mike waited patiently until Loren came on the line.

"Hey baby, I was just thinking about you," Loren said excitedly.

"I hope you were having wonderful thoughts about me like the ones I'm having about you."

"Whew, you have no idea," she replied while fanning herself.

"That's what I like to hear sweetheart. I was calling to

see if this was going to be a late night for you. If not I'm thinking Chinese food, movies and you tonight."

"I think I am going to have a late night. I just received a major shipment in today for four different jobs I'm working on. I need to get things catalogued and separated. The two local projects will need to be loaded up in the truck so that my assistants can deliver those. There were some serious mix-ups in some samples I received for two clients coming in tomorrow and I haven't put their portfolios together yet of my plans for their new offices, so yes it looks like it's a late night for me and I'm already exhausted. I'm going to let everyone go home early so that we can get an early start tomorrow, but I'll be here sort of late. I'm sorry because you know I really wanted to see you and spend time with you tonight."

Mike was concerned hearing how overwhelmed she was with work.

"Loren, you need to slow down some. You're going to wear yourself out."

"I know. I missed my spa treatment this week which normally helps me get relaxed when my week gets crazy. I seem to have so much going on at one time. I told you about that job I have going on in Barbados. I finally received the shots of the layouts for the lobby and now that everything is complete and I've everything shipped, I'm going to need to take a trip there to be sure everything is ready for the re-grand opening at the end of next week. Having a quiet night with you sounds so wonderful, but I still have so much to do here at the office."

"Don't worry sweetheart. We'll do it another night. I know how it is to have so much that you need to have done in a short period of time. We can definitely do this another night."

"Thank you," Loren said. "You are the best. I'll call you later?"

"Call me when you need a break."

Mike disconnected the line after talking to Loren. He was genuinely concerned that she was doing too much. She had a lot to do and at the same time, he felt like she needed some relaxation as well. He had a plan in mind and put in a call to Jason, his favorite supper club owner.

"Hey Jase."

"Mike, what's up man?"

"I need a favor. Here is what I need."

Mike gave him a rundown of what he needed him to do.

~~

Loren could feel that every muscle in her body was tight and every bone ached. She had been busy at work since the wee hours of the morning. It was now nine o'clock at night and she still had a lot to do. Her staff had left a few hours ago and she was thankful for their dedicated work. If it had not been for them, she wouldn't be as far ahead as she was with organizing portfolios for new projects and getting displays of new samples ready for setup in the lobby of her shop. Her displays were small scale examples of how the space in a room could be used more efficiently. It wasn't just about colors and furniture. It was more about how to place the furniture and the best colors to use for the space depending on what the customer wanted to use the room for. Once she set up a small scale design of a room for them, she worked out a budget that includes product, supplies and workman hours. She loved what she did, but there were times when it was exhausting and today was one of those days, she thought. She was upset that she wouldn't get to see Mike tonight. They got to spend so little time together as it was and she liked having him to herself whenever possible.

She was about to work on the next display case when she heard a knock on the locked door to the business. She went closer to see who would be showing up at this hour and saw Mike standing on the other side.

What was he doing here? she thought. She opened the door to let him in and noticed him carrying an armload of items, including a picnic basket.

"Mike, what are you doing here? I thought you were going home for the evening," she said.

Mike walked past her into the lobby.

"I was and then I decided that you needed a break and I'm sure dinner as well, so I thought I'd come and bring you both."

She got a closer look at everything he was carrying. Besides the picnic basket, he was carrying a couple of blankets, a pillow and a large bag that appeared to be full of items as well. Her heart swelled knowing how much he cared about her.

"Michael Bailey, what is running through that head of yours and what's in this bag and the basket?" she said, trying to get a look inside each one.

"Lock the door Loren and follow me."

Mike already knew his way around, having been to her shop many times. He found his way to the rear of the shop to find the perfect spot for a night of romance.

Loren watched as he started moving things around to make a clearing. She stood silently while he laid the blankets down, then the pillow. He opened the bag first and took out candles, an IPod with speakers which he plugged in and put on some soft jazz music; her favorite of course. He then reached back into his bag of tricks and pulled out a short, silk white robe for her and a black one for him and several massage oils and towels, placing them on the blanket. She then watched as he removed two bottles of wine, one white and one red, from the basket along with some freshly sliced fruit, containers of Chinese food and two hefty slices of apple pie, another of her favorites. When he was done removing the rest of the items, he turned to her.

"Loren, I know you have a lot of work to do tonight and I'm not trying to distract you from that, but I wanted to help you relax. You sounded stressed on the phone so for a few hours, I'm going to help take your mind off of work while I give you a massage, followed by a delicious dinner. Then I'm going to stay and help you finish up whatever work you have to do."

She couldn't believe what he had taken the time to do for her tonight. She was speechless.

"Thank you," was all she could get out without shedding tears of joy.

Loren went to Mike, placed her arms around his waist and leaned into him, loving the closeness she now realized she needed from him all day.

Mike kissed her forehead and handed her a robe.

"Now, go into your office bathroom, remove everything and put this robe on. In the meantime, I'm going to finish setting everything up."

Loren excitedly did as he asked, being more than grateful for him.

When she returned, she found him sitting on the blanket in his black robe, surrounded by lit candles. He had turned off all of the other lights so that the candles would cast a romantic glow in the room.

When Mike saw Loren enter, he couldn't help but notice how exotic she looked in the candlelit space. He was happy that he decided to do this for her tonight.

"I want you to lay down flat on the blanket. You can take your robe off."

Loren was already getting turned on at the romantic atmosphere he'd set up.

He whispered in her ear, "No thoughts of sex tonight baby. You know I can read your expressions. My plan is to focus on getting you totally relaxed. We'll save the sex for another night. Tonight is all about romance."

Loren felt a chill, a shiver as he spoke. He was crazy if he thought he was going to set all this up and tease her. She would wait to see how the night played out.

She laid down on the blanket while Mike grabbed the oil, straddled her legs and started massaging her neck, then her shoulders. She was already feeling relaxed as he began working the kinks out with his magnificent hands.

While he continued to relax her, Loren could only think of how thankful she was for a man who was as thoughtful as he was, even if she couldn't tell anyone about it. Just like tonight, he'd always shown her that he was always thinking about her. She would get deliveries of flowers or come out to get in her car and find a card or a note from him. He did lots of things to make her feel special and tonight was another she could add to the list.

Mike could feel when Loren finally started to relax. He began to sing to her softly as his thoughts turned to how appreciative he was for this beautiful woman whom he would do anything for and grateful for a great friend who put all of this together for him with just a phone call. He continued to massage her as watched her close her eyes and as he felt all tension dissipate from her body. This was his one and only plan for the evening.

Chapter 14

Loren was ecstatic that things had actually worked out between her brother Duron and Taija. She was concerned at one time when it appeared they weren't going to be able to repair the damage done to the relationship due to miscommunication.

Duron had spotted Taija's ex-boyfriend at her house and assumed the two had resumed their relationship. Now that things were finally cleared up, she couldn't be happier for them. She was thrilled that today, her brother was marrying Taija and she was serving as one of two maids of honor. The other was Taija's friend Victoria from Boston. She was also looking forward to seeing Mike at the wedding since he was serving as one of the groomsmen.

They had been secretly seeing each other for over six months and so far other than Taija and Jase, who agreed to keep their secret, no one else has realized they had something going on.

Even with the happy occasion taking place, she felt saddened because after a few delay, Mike was finally making his move to California and didn't expect the rush of emotions that flowed through her every time they talked about his move.

She had taken additional trips to the west coast, first to do a walk-through of the house that was just about completed, with the exception of some add-ons he wanted from the contractor and then to continue with her designs for the finished spaces.

She loved her trips their where the beaches were beautiful and she could do her own star gazing. She was tickled when she decided to shop on Rodeo drive one day and literally bumped into Denzel Washington. It never mattered to her how much older than her he was, he was still the finest man she had ever set eyes on, well that is except for her baby Mike. None compared to him.

She couldn't wait to see him later today. She knew he was going to be the finest brother in the place in his tuxedo. This was the second time they would be at a major function with her entire family and they had to watch their interaction. She still wasn't ready to tell anyone that they were seeing each other. Everything was going great and she didn't want to rock the boat. She did have to admit that things between the two of them were better than she ever thought they would be. He treated her like a queen and he put his all into letting her know that she was everything to him. If it were up to Mike, everyone would know.

He had been pushing her more lately to come clean with her family. He was ready to deal with the backlash that he knew he would get from her brother Duron, but he was ready for it. Mike had been telling her that even Duron had been sensing something different about him and that he had not noticed Mike with any women lately. He assumed Mike was either getting tired of the womanizing or that Mike was so busy with work, that he didn't make as much time for pleasure as he had in the past.

He was preparing to move to the west coast soon and she knew that when Duron inquired about his personal life and he had nothing to tell him, he figured it was due to the move and never drilled him on it. Even now, knowing how well things were going, she wasn't ready for anyone to know. They had some issues to work out.

Loren expressed her concern about some of the women Mike had been casually involved with. Though she believed him when he said he hadn't been seeing any of them, there was one in particular that didn't want to accept that he was no longer interested. She also knew of his very active sex life and wanted to be sure he didn't have desires that she didn't know about. She believed in keeping things fresh and new and knowing how high his sex drive was, she wanted to be sure she was fulfilling all of his needs. He assured her, she was all he needed.

Mike shared with her about this one woman that he had been seeing for a while. Though they were not having a relationship, they had fallen into a pattern of satisfying each other's needs and doing so often. This woman named Shelly still continued to contact him as if he had never told her he was no longer interested. Mike assured her Shelly was no issue, but even after a lot of time has passed, she was still trying to be a part of Mike's life. Loren figured what had occurred between Shelly and Mike was much deeper for Shelly than it was for Mike. She decided to let him handle it and she trusted him when he said it was over between them. One thing Loren knew was that women did not let go as easily as men. She knew what a great catch Mike was and she was sure this Shelly woman knew as well.

She removed all thoughts of Mike and any other woman from her mind as she continued getting ready for the wedding.

~~

The seven weeks following her brother's wedding was a very busy time for Loren. She was preparing for another trip to the west coast to work out some design finalities with Mike's house. Completing the work on the office turned out to be easier than she thought. The house was another story. It was large and very beautiful. She had to convince Mike to brighten up some of the rooms and to get away from the plain, dull colors men often wanted.

Since her flight was very early the next, she decided to stop by her parent's house beforehand. When she pulled up to the house, she saw her oldest brother Jake's car in the driveway. She also noticed the car seats in the back which meant her niece and nephew were with him. She loved Lyric and Milo as if they were her very own. She couldn't wait to see them again. Lyric had served as a flower girl at her brother's wedding and Milo was the ring carrier. They looked cute all dressed up for the affair.

"Anybody home?" Loren hollered into the house as she entered.

"We're in the kitchen, Loren," her mother shouted as she came through the door.

When she reached the kitchen, her mother, brother and sister-in-law, Kim were sitting at the kitchen table looking at pictures from the wedding.

"Hey everybody!"

"Hey," they all chimed at the same time.

"Let me see the pictures when you're finished."

"Look at them fast Loren. We've been here a while with mom and dad and we were about to leave. Kim wants to get the photos in a nice book for Duron and Taija and we need to get them to the photographer today," her brother stated.

"Okay, I'm not staying long either. I still have some packing to do and my flight is early in the morning."

Loren's mother looked up at her, from viewing the pictures.

"I really don't like you taking these flights to California by yourself. It's not safe for a young woman to be traveling there alone."

"Mom, I'm going to be fine. I'll only be gone a few days and besides, Mike will be there this time. He flew out this morning to take care of some business and will meet me at the house tomorrow to go over some last minute ideas I have. I'll be fine so don't worry."

"When is Mike actually moving? I hear things are just about ready," Jake asked.

Loren loved talking about Mike. She hoped her over excitement didn't show.

"First, where are my niece and nephew? I saw the car seats?"

"They're with dad in the back yard. He's having a mini playground built and they wanted to watch the men set it up."

"Okay, I'll say hi to them in a few minutes. To answer your question, Mike has another couple of weeks before he actually moves. The project starts in about three months and he wants to be completely settled by then. It's exciting and you should see the new offices they are opening. I'm planning to fly back out with Duron and Taija for the grand opening in a few weeks. Speaking of the newlyweds, has anyone heard from them since they got back from the honeymoon?"

Her mother answered.

"Yes, they stopped by last week for a quick visit. They were still in the midst of moving the rest of Taija's things from her place to the house. They've also been adjusting to being back at work. Besides that, I think they've been hibernating like newlyweds should."

Loren had no doubt that they were.

"Well I'll catch them when I get back in town."

She flipped through the pictures while everyone talked around her. When she finished, she stopped to give her niece and nephew a quick hug and then left so that she could finish her packing.

As she drove, she couldn't help but think of the conversation she and Mike had earlier in the day. He was getting frustrated that months later, they were still sneaking around. He felt that enough time had passed and that she needed to decide if they were going to work out or not. He would be moving soon and he wanted their relationship established openly before he left. To him there was no doubt. He knew she didn't have doubts that they would work out. She just couldn't find the right words to have the conversation with her brother and she knew she needed to tell him first. He knew the longer they waited, the angrier Duron would be.

The last week or so they had both been busy that the subject didn't come up until today. He wanted to be free to visit her in Atlanta and to have her visit him in California without the cover of a lie. His house would soon be finished and there would be no need for her to continue her trips out. How would she explain it then? Loren didn't know. Right now things were going well for them and she didn't want to rock the boat, not with his move on the horizon.

Loren had made Mike a promise that if he let her get through this trip, she would tell Duron when she got back to Atlanta. He was back from his honeymoon and he and Taija were busy enjoying their new married life. She didn't want to bring up anything that would cause drama. She asked him to be patient with her for a little while longer. Of course he gave in, as he always did, but he told her after this trip out to California, if she didn't tell Duron, then he was going to tell him. She knew Mike was of dragging out the inevitable. He had done a good job proving to her what being in a relationship with him would be like. He had proved he could be faithful to her and deep down, she agreed with him that they were made to be together. She would talk to Duron when she got back and however things turned out, she and Mike were ready to deal with it, together.

Chapter 15

"Taija are you sure you're going to be okay if I fly out to California to take a look at how the new office is coming along? I know you've been sick and I don't want to leave you."

"Duron I'm fine. It's morning sickness and it's natural. I'm only six weeks along and I'll be fine. I still can't believe I got pregnant on our honeymoon. I thought it would take a while for me to get pregnant after being off of birth control just one month."

Duron was shocked as well.

"I told you I was ready to start our family as soon as you were and it looks like our sooner came very soon. You've made me the happiest man around," he said pulling his wife into his arms.

"I'm happy too and wasn't sure what I would continue to feel once the doctor confirmed my pregnancy, but I've been extremely happy and excited even with the morning sickness. Don't worry about me, I'll be fine while you're gone. Remember Victoria is coming in from Boston for a few days for a meeting and she'll be around while you're gone so stop worrying."

"Okay babe. This is my first baby so I don't know what to expect. All I see is you running to the bathroom to throw-up at the mention of food. If you say its normal, then I'll go with that, but if you need me, I'll be a cell phone call away and I'm glad Victoria will be here with you just in case."

Duron kissed his wife as if he were experiencing his last supper. He knew he would never get enough of kissing her. He couldn't believe that after all they went through, she was now his wife and was pregnant with their first baby. They agreed to wait before telling their families. Taija wanted to tell Victoria because she knew Victoria would figure it out during her visit if Taija continued to suffer from morning sickness. Still, he had reservations about leaving her for a few days to fly to California. He couldn't do much to help lessen the effects of the morning sickness, but he liked being able to get her ginger ale and crackers to calm her stomach and keep a cold wash cloth handy to wipe her forehead.

As the kiss began turning into more than just a casual kiss, Taija pushed Duron away, knowing if they continued he would miss his flight.

"That's enough lover boy. Get going before you miss your flight. Did you call Mike to let him know you were visiting the California office while he's out there too?"

Duron continued packing.

"No I didn't. I'll stop by the office and catch him when I get there. It's early in the morning right now in California, too early to call him. He knew I would be coming out soon; I just didn't tell him when. I want to go now because I have several big meetings coming up that I need to be here for and I won't be able to get away again anytime soon."

"Have fun with Victoria this week. I'll call you when I land to check on you. If you're still going in the office this afternoon, don't overdo it. My baby basting in the oven wants you to take things slow and easy."

Duron leaned over to kiss Taija's still flat stomach though he knew his child was growing daily. He couldn't wait to meet him or her. It didn't matter to him what they were having as long as the baby was healthy and looked like his beautiful wife.

"I love you babe," Duron said heading out of the door.

"Love you too," Taija hollered at his back as he left.

~~

Loren and Mike were finally stirring after a night of love making that left them exhausted. As daylight began to pour through the windows of Mike's house, Loren moved to get up first. As she was about to put her feet on the floor, Mike reached over and pulled her back towards him, kissing her shoulder blades as he pulled her back down on the bed. He attempted to roll her under him for what Loren assumed was another round of passion.

"Not so fast. You've had me trapped in this bed all night long and remember there comes a time when a body has to relieve itself and my time is now. I have to go, so let go."

Loren heard Mike laugh as he let her go and watched as she ran to the bathroom.

After she closed the bathroom door, he leaned back on his pillow and thought about how happy he was. He was glad he was able to have Loren with him in California and not just for work purposes. He loved that she was invested in making sure the interior of his home was exactly how he wanted it to be, but he wanted time with her where they were not talking about work. He only wished they didn't have to continue to keep their relationship a secret from her family. It was getting tricky and complicated finding time to spend together, especially when they were in Atlanta. He was running out of excuses of why he would suddenly start showing up at Knight family functions, more than he usually would. Luckily her family had always considered him family so it wasn't odd for him to be around as much as he had been lately.

He was happy that they could go out publicly and go on actual dates, kiss in public if they felt like it and enjoy each other's company without having to look over their shoulders wondering if anyone spotted them. He was worried that soon things would get even more complicated with his move. Loren had promised him that she would talk to her brother when she got back to Atlanta. He wanted to be there with her for the conversation so that he could help Loren explain the long term secrecy. She wanted to do it on her own and he was going to respect her wishes. All he knew was that soon, he would be free to love her anytime and anyplace he wanted. If there were any reservations from her family, he had no problem reassuring them that he wanted Loren and he would do anything for her and anything to keep her.

Loren needed a hot shower. Her body ached, in a good way from the passion that she and Mike shared throughout the night. They can't seem to get enough of each other. It wasn't just the sex either. For years she knew him as Mike, Duron's best friend, but now she gets to know Mike on a more personal level and everything she's learning about him she likes. They have a lot in common.

They both love football and are die hard Baltimore

Ravens fans even though he's from New York and she's from Atlanta, two cities that also have their own football teams. Who couldn't love a team that had Ray Lewis?

They each love scary movies and the scarier the better. She didn't always like them, but now that they were together, she loved being scared around him knowing that when she reached out in the night, he was there to soothe her.

Loren exited the bathroom after her shower to find Mike in the same position she'd left him in. He was giving her that look that let her know that he would rather she joined him back on the bed instead of him getting out of it. She could see something making a tent of the blanket on the bed, an obvious sign that he had sex in mind. The man was an animal, always ready and didn't need a break or a nap in between. His sexual appetite was insatiable and she was more than happy to accommodate his every desire.

"So I see what you have in mind for us this morning," she said looking at him with the same lust-filled look he was giving her.

Mike never said a word. He simply pulled the blanket off to show her he was already throbbing, hard and waiting just for her and that's all the invitation she needed.

Loren dropped her towel.

Mike knew he would never tire of seeing Loren in all of her gloriously nakedness. Just the sight of her sent his pulse spiraling out of control. He watched as she took her time, seducing him with her sexy walk towards the bed. When she reached him, he reached out and pulled her to him, tumbling her down on the bed. It never amazed Mike just how unglued he became around her. His body had come to know hers so well and was always ready to mate with hers.

Loren was enjoying the kissing and caressing, but at her current heightened state of arousal, she wanted more. In between Mike kissing and caressing her, she uttered, "Condom, now Mike!"

After Mike sheathed himself, he rejoined Loren on the bed. When he covered her body with his, Loren rocked her body into his letting him know she was ready. When she spread her legs, he answered the invitation and entered her body in one long, hard push.

He knew he wasn't going to last long when Loren started muttering that she wanted him to go faster, that she needed more, that she needed it harder. Her musings sent Mike's love making to an all new level of raw abandonment. His thrusts were firm and deep and Loren matched him stroke for stroke. They were both surging to completion. They were dancing to the sound of music that only the two of them could make.

Every nerve ending in Loren's body was on fire. She was clawing, clawing, clawing to let go. She urged him on with her sighs of pleasure. She couldn't help, but say his name over and over again. She needed him to know what he was doing to her and that she loved all of it. She knew what was at the end of the race and she needed it. She could only feel this way with Mike. His moans of her name were her undoing as she experienced an out of body experience. Her release shook her entire body as if she were going through convulsions.

It was only after Loren was satiated that Mike allowed himself to join her as he shuddered through his potent release.

Loren felt his orgasm and helped prolong his pleasure

by clinching and tightening her muscles around him as he continued to fill her with his unrestrained passion.

This release for Mike was blinding. He could feel the pulsing behind his eye lids as he waited for his body to calm after the raging storm he'd just experienced. He couldn't speak, he couldn't move, he couldn't do anything, but kiss Loren over and over because what they shared went beyond mere words. If things were always going to be like this between them, he was ready to sign up to be on board for life.

~~

Duron landed at the airport and headed straight to the new office to see how far the construction had come along. He appreciated the pictures Mike had been sending him, but he wanted to see everything for himself.

After picking up his rental, he drove straight to the site. There was a three hour time difference than where he boarded in Atlanta so it was actually eleven o'clock in the morning and he was happy to see the men busy at work, diligently working to meet the deadline of when they needed the office up and running. The project they were obligated to begin was on a tight schedule and if they were going to begin, they needed the office space to work out of up and running as well. From what he could see, things were moving along very well. He exited his vehicle and went in search of Mike. Not finding him, he asked around for the foreman.

"I'm Duron Knight, one of the partners here at Pioneer. Looks like your men are making good time, which is great. Any chance you've seen Michael Bailey, one of the other owners around here today?"

The foreman thanked him for complimenting the men

on the work done so far.

"I haven't seen Mr. Bailey around yet today. He did mention he may be around a little later than usual today. The final work was done on his house yesterday so I believe he was hanging around there today to be sure everything was to his liking."

"Great, I'll head over there and get my first look at this west coast mansion I've been hearing he'll be living in. I'll be around later and I'd appreciate it if you could make the time to walk me around the complex and show me what still needs to be done when I return."

"Yes sir. I'll be here all day," the foreman said.

Duron shook hands with him and headed back to his car while dialing Mike's cell phone to let him know he was in California.

Mike didn't answer his phone even after he tried reaching him a few times. He decided to leave a message to let him know he was in town and was on his way out to the house. He entered the address in the GPS and hoped Mike was there when he got there.

~~

Mike and Loren were enjoying a breakfast of champions at his new black marble island in his newly redesigned kitchen. Her only attire was one of his t-shirts that was three sizes too big for her, but she liked being in his shirts. Mike was still walking around in the towel he had donned after coming out of the shower after their last session of early morning marathon lovemaking. They were careful to stay in the kitchen area since they were clad in little clothing. There were still members of the construction crew around working on the lower level of the house doing finishing touches.

"We are so domesticated, Mike," Loren said while enjoying her western omelet and buttermilk pancakes.

Mike muffled some type of response, trying to talk with his mouth full of food.

She laughed at his attempt to eat and talk, finally swallowing he replied.

"Does this domesticated scene scare you?" he asked.

"Not at all. I'm starting to get use to what we have."

"Enough to finally let your family know about us?"

He could see his comment surprised her. He hated that he needed to constantly remind her that it was time to let go of the secret and tell everyone. He was determined to get it resolved.

"I told you I would tell them when I got back and I will."

She nervously bit her lip and Mike knew there was more.

"I hear reservation and I see it in your face and in the way you're nibbling on your lip. What is it?"

"I may not tell them as soon as I get back. I want to feel them out first, but I promise I will. I'm going to start with my mom and she what she thinks the others will say, especially Duron. She knows all of us better than we know ourselves. I just don't want to rush into it."

"Rush Loren? It's been months and I wouldn't call that rushing at all. In fact, I see you stalling and I don't understand why you still have a problem with this. Do you still think I'm seeing other women? You think I'm not serious about wanting to commit to you? To us? If that's the case you're wrong. I'm not seeing anyone else, nor do I want to. I think I have proven myself beyond all of the reservations you had in the beginning about my ability to be with just you and no other women."

"I don't have reservations about you at all. I trust that you meant what you said when you said you wanted to prove to me that you wanted me and only me. My one and only issue is still the reaction from Duron. I love what you and I have. I am ready to share it with the world. I just want to do it the right way."

Mike interrupted her, pissed off.

"What is the right way? I think it's coming clean with him and everyone else, give them time to deal with it and we can show them what we mean to each other. We're not some dirty little secret. We're adults who have made a decision to be together despite anything else. Either you are on board with this or you're not."

Mike knew his anger was showing, but he didn't care. This secret affair was ridiculous to him and he wanted her to know. He was losing patience with the entire situation. He didn't understand what the big deal was. She was no longer a young girl who needed her big brother's approval when it came to dating. He could handle anything Duron brought his way. He didn't think it was as serious as Loren was making it out to be. The more he thought about everything, his anger began boiling over. He pushed his plate away after no longer having an appetite.

"You are a grown woman. You do not need your family's buy-in for a relationship with me or anyone else. I understand that initially Duron may have a problem with our relationship and that would be based on what he knows about my personal dating life. I also believe that he would know that I wouldn't casually date you. I want to see where our relationship will go without any barriers. I think your brother would be angrier at the fact that we have been seeing each other for months now and we have been keeping it a secret. I can see him now believing that we've kept this a secret because I wanted it and not because you wanted it. We're men, it's how we think. I think we should just tell him and get it over with. The rest of your family wouldn't be a problem. I respect that you want to protect me and what we have from the wrath of Duron, but for this to be what we both want and deserve without having to hide, we have to get this out in the open. Sneaking around is getting more and more complicated the more time we try to spend together. I will be moving soon and I want this out in the open for everyone to celebrate what we have together."

Loren knew he was right. This has gone on long enough. She was being unfair to him, getting him to go along with this for so long. She was proud to be involved with him and wanted everyone to know about it.

"Okay baby, you're right, but let me tell him okay. I want to be able to reassure him that I know what I'm doing getting involved with you and that you are not using me just for a casual fling. He needs to know that this is not casual and that I'm in love with you."

She stopped cold at her own declaration. She didn't realize it until the words were already out of her mouth. She knew how she felt, but she didn't intend to blurt it out like that. She looked at Mike to try and determine if she'd caught him off guard with her confession of love and if he embraced it or showed any sign that he wanted to run from the room and never come back. The silence was scary, especially since the look on his face showed he heard her but he had yet to say anything. She wasn't even sure he was still breathing, he was so still. There was no facial expression beyond the blank stare looking back at her. She was about to speak when he spoke first.

"I love you too. I'm in love with you, Loren and I have been for a long time. I think I fell in love with you years ago and fought that feeling, but I don't want to anymore. I love you baby; I love you so much."

Loren wanted to cry. Everything she ever wanted and needed was standing inches away from her. How could she have ever made the decision to keep this kind of love away from her family. She wanted to shout to the world that they were in love and she didn't care what anyone thought about it. She watched as he closed the distance between them by coming around to her side of the counter. She smiled as he picked her up and sat her on top of the counter as he occupied the space between her legs.

This, Mike thought, is where he always wanted to be. In the arms of the woman he loved for the rest of his life and he didn't care who had a problem with it. Their love would overcome any obstacle including family or friends who may object. Deep down, he had a feeling none of them would. No words were needed as he braced her face in his hands and kissed her, not with softness or tenderness, but with fierce abandonment and deep intensity that left no room for doubt of his feelings for her. He pulled her closer as she leaned into the kiss, wrapped her legs around his waist and pulled him as close as she could to her and kissed him back with a fierceness that left little room for doubt that their love would conquer anything.

~~

Duron pulled up to Mike's new house and was impressed by what he saw. The house wasn't as big as he thought it would be, but it was still pretty big for one person. He was about to ring the doorbell when the front door opened and a man in overalls greeted him as they almost bumped into each other.

"Excuse me," the worker said.

"I'm looking for Mike, is he around?"

"Sure. My guys and I were just finishing up laying the carpet on the lower level and I think I heard Mr. Mike and his guest in the kitchen."

So Mike was already christening every room of his house, Duron thought to himself.

"Typical Mike," he said. "I'll just go on in and make my presence known."

"Okay with me," the worker said as he exited the house. Duron entered and found his way to the kitchen. The scene before him didn't surprise him. It appeared Mike was busy at work on a woman he had hoisted up on the island in his kitchen. They were deep in a kiss that Duron was sure was on its way to something else if he had not come in and was about to interrupt them.

"Uh, excuse me for interrupting," Duron said as he made his way further into the kitchen.

The visitor startled Mike and Loren and when he released her lips and turned around, his heart stopped beating when he realized he was face to face with Duron. He knew the moment Duron realized who the woman was behind him. When he did, the air left the room; no one said a word.

Loren didn't move when she realized it was her brother. Knowing she needed to get down off of the island where Mike had placed her, she slid down and stayed behind Mike.

Time seemed to stand still as Duron looked from Mike to Loren then back to Mike again. He wasn't sure that his eyes weren't playing tricks on him. He had to be imagining that he just saw Mike and his sister caught in a lip lock with Mike in a towel and Loren scantily clad in an oversized t-shirt, hopefully with something on underneath.

"What the hell is this?" Duron said, laced with intense anger. He stepped a little closer to Mike and asked again.

"What the hell is going on here?"

Loren and Mike tried to answer at the same time, with Mike over-talking her.

"Duron, bro, just calm down," he said with his hands up in a show of surrender.

"What the hell are you talking about calm down? Tell me that is not my sister standing behind you and I will calm down," Duron said through clenched teeth, seething.

Duron was about to explode and that frightened Loren. Her greatest fear was about to happen unless she did something. She made her way out of Mike's shadow and came around to his side.

"D, just wait a minute. I know what you see, but let me explain."

Duron looked down at his sister and all he could think about was the many, many stories he and Mike had swapped over the years about all the women they had bedded and he was furious. All he could think was, no Mike was *not* screwing his sister like she was one of those playthings he was known to hook up with.

"Explain, Lo? Explain what? So you and Mike? How long has this been going on?"

"D, just calm down and listen to me okay? We've been seeing each other for a little while now. Actually it's been quite a few months. I'm sorry we didn't tell you, but we needed to be sure we really wanted this before we told anyone. This isn't some casual affair; it's much more than that and I hope you'll come to accept our relationship."

Loren was talking to Duron, but he was looking directly at Mike with a death stare.

"I don't hear you Lo. I don't hear my sister standing in front of me almost naked with a man I consider a brother. I don't hear you."

While he talked, Duron never took his eyes off of Mike. He had no doubt Mike was reading his thoughts and knew that no amount of explanations was going to alleviate the distrust that was now surrounding their friendship. He also knew having Loren in her current state of undress and he in only a towel wasn't helping the situation. They needed to talk and they needed to do it without Loren present. His worst nightmare was coming true; he had been caught with his best friend's sister and neither he nor Loren had warned him that it was going on. Mike saw the hurt, the disappointment and the anger that was at a boiling point.

"Duron, please say something or at least look at me. This really isn't what you think it is," Loren continued to explain.

"Lo, I've already told you I don't hear you," he said, again not looking at her, but keeping his burning eyes on Mike.

"Loren, why don't you go upstairs and put on some clothes and let me talk to Duron."

She looked from him to Duron and the looks passing between the two of them scared her beyond anything she'd ever experienced. She was afraid to leave them alone, not knowing what would happen.

"I'm not leaving until we talk this out."

"Loren, please go upstairs and let me talk with Duron. It's going to be fine, but you need to go and leave us alone to talk," Mike pleaded, still not taking his eyes off of Duron who was getting angrier by the minute.

She knew he was right. For starters she couldn't remain standing in front of her brother almost naked and clearly the conversation needed to be between the two of them. She could talk to Duron later. This situation was her fault, making the decision to keep her relationship with Mike a secret and now it was blowing up in her face. The two people she loved the most were at odds and only the two of them could fix it. She didn't say another word as she walked around her brother, who never turned to look at her, and she walked off in the direction of the stairs.

When Loren was out of range, Duron started first. His plan was to keep his voice down, but what came could have shattered the windows of the house.

"Mike, my sister man? Really? There weren't enough women in Atlanta that you had to move on to my sister?"

Mike didn't come back at him with anger, knowing Duron had every right to be upset. I wanted to diffuse the situation and he couldn't do that if they both shouted in rage.

"It's not like that."

"It's not like what, Mike? It's not like you haven't been leaving a trail of broken hearts all over Atlanta? It's not like I don't know how you go from woman to woman, using them for the pleasure of it? Or is it that I don't know how you get what you want from women then move on to the next one?"

"Duron, first calm down man. I am not using your sister. I'm in love with her and I have been for some time now. This is not just some casual, sexual affair that you are used to knowing me to have. I love Loren with every fiber of my being."

"Mike, man do not talk about sex and my sister in the same sentence. This is my sister!"

Mike could see the veins in Duron's forehead look as if they're about to pop. He had never seen him this angry before. He knew he had every right to be, he just hoped he could convince him this wasn't casual.

"D, you know me. I know you know my history with women and yes you have first-hand knowledge of my sexual prowess over the years, but like I said, that's not what's going on here. Did you hear me? I said I'm in love with her. You know I've never made that declaration before, not even in my younger years to get a woman in bed. I've never said it before, but I'm telling you right now I love your sister."

"Right, you mentioned love. Love? You love my sister? You don't know anything about loving a woman. You go through so many women that I don't even think you even remember their names. This is sick and disappointing, especially coming from you. You don't love my sister. You don't know the meaning of the word. What I do know is it looks like you screwed my sister, have been doing so for a while now and I walked in on you about to do it again on a kitchen counter. Are you crazy? My sister isn't one of your sex kittens. What the hell are you thinking?"

Mike understood Duron's anger. He knew that his anger was not about the fact that he and Loren were together, it was about the fact that all Duron ever saw Mike do was bed one woman after the other without feeling. He needed Duron to know that was not the case here.

"I'm not using your sister Duron. I meant it when I said I'm in love with her."

Mike watched as Duron turned his anger into pacing back and forth.

"Love? You love her enough to sneak around with her? Is there some reason why you felt the need to keep this a secret? The only reason I can think of is that you wanted to get what you wanted until you were through then walk off like you often do with women."

Mike tried to explain the rationale behind not telling anyone without putting the blame on Loren since she was the one who wanted to keep things a secret. He couldn't seem to get a word in as Duron spouted off with anger.

"You know what? My sister is a grown woman and she can be involved with whomever she wants. You on the other hand, Mike, work with me every day. We've been best friends for years and I am closer to you than I am to my own brothers. You could have told me; you should have told me!" he shouted.

"Duron I know."

He didn't get a chance to continue.

"I would have expected you to respect my sister more than to keep her a secret and have her sneaking around as if being with her was not worthy of being a public affair."

Mike started to explain himself and the situation, but Duron stopped him before he could say a word.

"Save it Mike. Whatever it is you were about to say you may as well save it for someone who gives a damn. Seeing you here with my sister like this is disturbing. I can't tell Loren who to or not to see or be with. I just wish she had not chosen you. Don't forget I know you. I know you just as well as you know yourself. Before I met and fell in love with Taija, you know who I was also. If you had a sister, would you want your sister hooking up with the Duron you knew back then? No you wouldn't because I was all about how many women I could bed, the pleasure in it without commitment of any kind and so are you."

Mike let Duron have his anger because he did understood it. It was his greatest fear when he and Loren decided to keep their affair a secret. He also knew Duron was right, he should have told him because it was the right thing to do. He let his desire for Loren overshadow what he knew was the right thing. He had played some wild mind games to get in women's pants and Duron was thinking that's what he was doing with Loren.

Disgusted with the situation, Duron turned to leave. Mike followed behind him and tried to stop him. When he reached him he grabbed his arm and Duron swung around furious.

"Don't touch me Mike. I'm serious man. It's taking everything I have in me to not lay you flat on this floor, so don't touch me. You're standing in my face in a towel, my sister had on a t-shirt and you were mauling her when I walked in the door. The last thing you want to do right now is stop me from leaving. If I stay, I'm not sure what I'll do.

Mike pulled his hand back and again raised them in surrender.

"D, man, don't leave like this. I know you're angry at me and I accept that. I'm sorry for this, but I'm not sorry for loving Loren. I won't apologize for that because I wasted a lot of time holding my feelings for her in check because of my friendship with you and I won't do that anymore. I love her and I hope after you've had a chance to calm down that you'll see this isn't a casual fling. We were concerned about your reaction and we wanted to tell you. Loren was going to tell you when she returned home. We didn't mean for things to turn out like this so please don't leave like this. Talk to your sister because I know she's upset. Talk to her and you will see that this is not a game I'm playing or running on her. We are in love."

Duron turned back toward the door. Before leaving he stopped, but didn't turn back around.

"You and Loren are two grown ass people. Do what you do. I'm just disappointed that the one man who knows me better than anyone I know would feel the need to hide this from me instead of coming to me like a man, like a best friend to let me know he was into my sister. Not that you owed it to me, but as my friend, as my best friend, I would have appreciated a heads up. I'm going to leave and head back over to the office park. Tell Loren I'll see her when she gets back to Atlanta."

Before Mike could say anything else, Duron left, slamming the door for added measure to show how pissed off he was.

Loren came down the stairs when she heard the door slam.

"I take it the conversation didn't go well?" she said, nibbling away nervously on her bottom lip.

"Not at all. I don't think he is as angry about the fact that we are seeing each other than he is about the fact that he found out about it by seeing you up on my kitchen counter and us sucking face like two animals in heat."

Loren needed to talk to Duron. She couldn't let him leave without them being able to talk. She needed to explain everything to him.

"I'm going to get my cell phone and call him. I can straighten this out. He needs to know that it was my idea to keep us a secret and not yours. I heard what he said to you. He thinks you kept me a secret so that you could get the sex you wanted then walk away with no one knowing about it. He needs to know that's not the case. You know how close he and I are. He has always been over protective of me. He was my rock when the one serious relationship I had tanked. He remembers the horrible state I was in following that and he worries about me."

Mike didn't think now was the time to talk to Duron.

"Loren just let him be for the moment. Why don't you wait until you get back home and talk to him in person? I think he needs time to cool off and approaching him with it right now won't help this at all. I've never seen him this angry and I don't want him taking his anger out on you when it's me he's angry with. I betrayed him as his best friend and that's something he and I need to work through. He loves you so he's not angry at you. You don't need to explain. This is something Duron and I are going to have to work through and I'll do that when I return to Atlanta. I'm going to give him the cooling off period I think he needs. This won't go away in a day and you trying to explain won't make him understand that we love each other. He's going to have to see it for himself. I don't plan to throw it in his face, but I don't plan to hide my love for you anymore; not from him and not from anyone else. I see what this has done to him and I don't want anyone else to feel cheated. Let him cool off and let me deal with this when I get back."

Loren nodded knowing he was right. She'd never seen her brother so angry and she never wanted to see it again.

For now, she'd let it go and try to talk to him when she returned to Atlanta.

She and Duron were the closest of her siblings and they never kept secrets from each other. She needed him to understand that her decision to not tell any of them about her relationship with Mike was to keep the peace until they could figure out where the relationship was going. They loved each other and Mike wasn't going to hurt her. The heat of the moment wouldn't allow her brother to see that, but she hoped with time, he'd come to understand and respect her decision. She just hoped that since this blew up in their face that it wouldn't hurt the relationship Duron and Mike had. She wasn't sure she could handle that.

Chapter 16

Loren was happy to be back home in Atlanta. She flew back alone, leaving Mike in California to finish up some business and to wait for the delivery of the rest of the furniture for his house. She had returned hoping to catch up with her brother. She found out from Mike that Duron didn't go back to the word site, but went back to the airport and caught a flight back home.

Now home in Atlanta, she decided to stop by his house before heading to her own place after landing. She pulled into the development where he and Taija lived. When she pulled up to the house, she felt nervous, hoping her conversation with Duron didn't become confrontational. She knew how overprotective he could be and she wanted to remind him that she was old enough to handle her own affairs and she didn't need him handling things for her.

She didn't use her key to enter the house. Now that Taija and Duron were now under one roof, she had to respect their privacy and ring the bell like any other guest. She was excited when Taija opened the door. They had not seen each other since she and Duron had returned from their honeymoon.

"Loren, come on in. I'm so glad you stopped by."

"Hey Taija. You look good girl. Married life is already agreeing with you."

"Thanks, girl."

Loren followed Taija into the kitchen where she was making what looked like lunch.

"Can I get you anything to drink?" Taija asked Loren.

"No I'm good," she replied.

"I was making Duron and myself some lunch. He working from home today so I thought I'd surprise him with his favorite salmon salad and some fruit."

"I actually need to talk to Duron."

Taija looked at Loren with a sad look on her face.

"So he knows, huh Loren?"

She was thankful for Taija's friendship because as hard as it was for her to keep the secret, Taija never told Duron what was going on. She appreciated that.

"Yes, he does and thank you for not telling him, though I wished I had told him months ago. He caught Mike and I in what I will describe as an uncompromising position when he came to California."

"Loren, I had no idea you were in California with Mike or I would have warned you that he was coming. Even though you know I don't like to lie to your brother, I wouldn't want him to find out the way that he did. After all that mess with my ex-boyfriend, Keith, we promised no more secrets. The only reason I never said anything was because it's not my story to tell. I was hoping you and Mike would have told him and the family by now. It's been months and I know by now you two can see that you are meant to be together."

Loren knew Taija was right.

"I know and I'm sorry about how he found out, but I'm not sorry that he knows. I love Mike and it's time Duron stopped acting like my savior and let me live my own life, even if I decide that it's going to be with Mike."

Taija removed the cooked salmon from the indoor grill and placed it on top of Duron's salad. She then stopped what she was doing and looked over at Loren.

"You are still trying to decide if you are going to be with Mike, Loren? You just told me you are in love with him. What else is there to think about?"

Loren hunched her shoulders as if she didn't have an answer, but she did. She just didn't know if she should tell Taija about it. She didn't want to continue pouring more secrets that she'd want Taija to keep into her knowing that it could possibly cause trouble for her and Duron. After careful thinking, she decided to share a little about her reservations.

"Taija, I do love Mike. With everything that I am, I love him and he loves me and I don't doubt that at all. It's just that there is this woman that Mike had been seeing that bothers me."

Loren saw the shock on Taija's face.

"Bothers you? Do you mean the woman has been bothering you, literally, or the situation with this woman and Mike is bothering you?"

Loren looked nervously at the counter, not looking straight at Taija.

"Tai, where is Duron? I don't want him walking in on our conversation."

"He's down in the theater room, his man-cave. You know how he gets when he has a lot on his mind. When he came home yesterday, he told me what happened; well, not exactly what happened. He only told me that he caught you two together and he wasn't happy about it. I asked him what did you say and he said he hadn't talked to you yet. He talked with Mike and it didn't go over well and he didn't want to argue with you so he left California before talking to you."

"That he did Taija. I love my brother, but he's such a coward when it comes to me. He likes to dictate my life for me, but doesn't want to talk things out face to face with me. I'm going to talk to him before I leave here today."

Taija was happy to hear that. She didn't want to see a strain in her family.

"So tell me about this woman Loren."

"Okay, here it is. Mike, as you know, has never had a real relationship before becoming involved with me. He pretty much maintained friends with benefit type situations with women where it was mutually agreed that there were no strings attached. This one woman was not happy to hear that Mike would no longer be her bed buddy. At first Mike thought Shelly, that's her name, would be okay with it and when it was over they would both just walk away. We talked about her recently because I told him about this woman I kept seeing everywhere I went. I would go for coffee at the bagel shop or I'm leaving out of my office and I would see her parked nearby staring at me. As you know we don't go out together in the Atlanta area because we didn't want to run into anyone, so if we wanted to try a restaurant or do a movie, we would go several counties over and one evening he thought he saw her when we came out of the movie theater. He recognized her car, but when she saw that he noticed her, she sped off. It was no longer a coincidence. I asked him if he'd talked to her and he said he had."

Loren watched Taija's expression change from anger to worry.

"Wow Loren. This woman doesn't sound too stable. She appears to be stalking you both. You need to be careful. What is Mike saying about all this?"

"Again, he said he did tell her that they wouldn't be seeing each other anymore and that they had agreed it was a casual thing."

Taija continued making Duron's lunch while Loren spoke.

"I gave Mike my thoughts on how a woman would feel and think in these casual, benefit type situations. In their minds, they are in a relationship with the guy. No matter what they agreed to verbally, in a woman's head, she's involved. If she agrees to anything casual, it's because she's waiting for him to come around or she's waiting for him to be as into her as she is into him. She is thinking that it's only a matter of time. If the man find's her worthy as a bed partner, he will eventually want more and she's willing to wait until he comes to that realization."

Taija shook her head knowing Loren was right and realizing that men just didn't get it.

"Men have to realize women are emotional creatures and we base everything on feelings. No matter what we say out of our mouth's that we will go along with, it's not what we really feel. In the end, someone gets hurt and it's usually the woman."

Loren nodded in agreement.

"You are absolutely correct. I said all of that to Mike and he just keeps saying that Shelly knew the rules and she'll get over it. I'm just not so sure. I was half expecting to see her stalking us in California."

Taija looked up in shock.

"You didn't, did you?"

They both laughed.

"No, Taija. No California sightings. I'm just not sure she is over being with Mike as he would like her to be. He told me not to worry about it. He's going to talk to her again to be sure he's clear in his explanation that nothing further will be going on between them. I'll just let him handle it, but it doesn't mean I don't worry about it. You know a scorned woman can be hell on heels!"

Though Taija laughed, she knew that the entire situation could quickly get out of control if not resolved soon.

"Learn from my mistakes with your brother Loren and make sure this gets taken care of so that you two can move forward into the kind of happiness I have found."

Loren knew Taija was right.

"Speaking of my brother, I'm going to head down into the lion's den to talk to him. Wish me luck."

Taija didn't say anything. She just crossed her fingers and showed them to Loren so that she would know she's in her corner.

~ ~

Duron looked up as his sister entered his theater room and neither said a word. He looked from her back to the contracts he was reviewing. He knew sooner or later they'd have to have a conversation about what he walked in on. She was going to have to initiate the conversation.

Loren walked over and sat in one of the chairs in front of the theater screen in the last row, one row behind her brother.

"You know the last time we were in this room together, you were having problems with Taija?" Loren asked him, speaking to the back of his head.

"I do remember that," Duron replied.

"D, I'm sorry about not telling you about Mike and me. I know I should have, not because I had to, but because I don't like keeping secrets from you and Mike is your best friend."

"He's going to hurt you, you know that right?" Duron spoke without turning around to face her.

Loren could see this was not going to be an easy conversation.

"You don't know that and why would you say that?"

"I say it because I know Mike. He has done nothing but chase skirts for as long as he and I have been friends. He doesn't know anything else. Is that the kind of guy you're interested in?"

Loren was surprised to hear him say that about his friend.

"How can you say that about a man you call a brother?"

Duron wasn't trying to hurt her. He just wanted her to know what she was getting involved with.

"Do you remember how hurt you were when Sam hurt you by cheating on you? I will never forget how devastated you were. It almost killed me to see you in the state that relationship left you in."

He turned around to finally face Loren and talk to her face to face.

"I don't want you to think I don't like or love Mike like the brother I have always claimed him to be. I just know that he doesn't know what it means to really commit to a woman and he has never been able to have just one. I'm not trying to hurt you or talk down about him, it's just a fact."

Loren was crushed and she knew her faced showed the hurt at hearing Duron talk about Mike.

Duron could see his words were hurting Loren and that was not his intent. He got up and moved to sit in one of the chairs on the same row as Loren.

"Loren, what I saw when I walked into Mike's house, was what I usually see when I walk into a room with him and some woman; her with very little clothes on either just before or just after sex. It's always about the sex with him. I don't want to see him treat you the way I know he has treated other women. I'm not saying he's a horrible person, I'm simply saying I don't want my sister being a sex toy for any guy, especially not one that I'm so close with; in friendship and in business. If whatever you have doesn't work out, it could mean bad things all around; for you and him, for him and me, for him and this family."

Loren paused before she spoke. It was the one reason she didn't want anyone to know. She didn't want it to be an issue with Mike and her family and especially with Duron and Mike. She knew she should have come clean with them all about her relationship with Mike instead of being caught, almost with her panties down.

"D, I am in love with Mike and he is in love with me. I need you to support me on this. I need you to see that he is not the same anymore. We have been seeing each other for months now and it's been wonderful."

Loren saw the shock on his face.

"How many months? Since when Loren?" Duron asked.

"Since a little while after I started working on the designs for Mike's house. We just sort of hit it off. I will admit I have been interested in Mike for much longer than that. Our like for each other was mutual and then love blossomed from that."

Loren could see Duron wasn't convinced.

"D, he loves me, he really does. This is not a situation like what I went through with Sam. I learned a lot from that and I wouldn't set myself up for something like that again. He loves me. He is not that bed hopper you know. That's not him anymore. When was the last time you have heard him talk about any women, or seen him with any? Don't answer because I already know that answer. Not at all because that's not him anymore."

Duron could see how passionate Loren was about what she was saying.

"I'm sorry, D, but I'm only sorry that I kept this from you. I'm not sorry that I fell in love with your best friend. Please don't be mad at Mike because it wasn't his fault that we kept this from everyone. He wanted to tell you right away and I convinced him not to. I told him that I needed to be sure and I needed to be able to trust that I am what he wanted and before we told anyone and it didn't work out, I needed reassurance first. He told me from the beginning that we needed to tell everyone and he didn't want to keep it a secret, especially from you, so don't you dare fault him. Don't let this come between you two."

Loren leaned closer to Duron so that he could read her deepest thoughts. They have always been connected like that.

"I love him D. I love him so much and I need you to be okay with this because right now Mike is hurting. He's hurting because he can't get the look you had on your face out of his head or the hurt he heard in your words."

Duron could see that his support meant everything to Loren. She needed him by her side.

"D, do you remember who you used to be before you met Taija? You were no different than Mike was and look at you now. You can't even think of another woman you are so in love with her. I saw it and I stood in this very room and called you out on it because no matter what you were saying, I knew you were in love with her. I never said you couldn't be because you were too busy chasing skirts. I looked at you when you said her name, I saw you when the two of you were together and what I saw was a couple that was made to be together. That's what I have with Mike. It's love D. It's love."

Duron's heart melted when he saw tears form in Loren's eyes and she began to cry. He reached over and pulled her into a hug that only her favorite brother could give her.

"I love you Lo, you know that and I hear you. You and Mike are in love and I'm happy for you. If this is what you want, if Mike is what you want then I support you. I love you too much not to. I was just surprised and caught off guard by what I saw, but you're right. I was exactly who I said Mike was and when I met Taija, I couldn't imagine being with another woman. If Mike feels about you the way I feel about her, then yeah, I'd say you're both very much in love."

Duron felt much better when Loren looked up at him and smiled. She grabbed him tight around the neck and held on, thankful that he was going to be okay. She wished she had told him from the start and all of the drama could have been avoided.

"Thank you D. I love you."

"I love you too and I'll talk to Mike. We're good."

Loren looked at his face for reassurance.

"Really? Are you sure?"

"Yes, sis, I'm sure."

They both turned when they heard Taija enter the room with Duron's lunch.

"I see the two of you have made up. I'm glad because I was planning to lock you both in here until you figured this out."

"Yeah, we're good. Did you hear Taija? Loren and Mike are in love," Duron said.

Taija sat his lunch down and gave Loren a hug.

"Yeah, I heard and I'm happy for them. I know they'll be as disgustingly in love as you and I are."

Duron looked at them both.

"They better be or off with his head!"

"Now that this is over, I have to go. Work is calling and I need to unpack first," Loren said.

She gave Duron a hug and dashed for the door.

Taija turned to Duron after Loren left.

"I'm so proud of you. You know it was time to let Loren live her own life," Taija said.

Duron reached for his wife and pulled her into his lap so that she straddled him.

"You're right and I'll deal with your punishment later because I also figured out that you knew all along and didn't tell me," Duron chuckled while nuzzling her neck.

Taija immediately felt a fire begin in the pit of her stomach and an arousal began in between her legs. She slid a little closer to that part of him that began to rise and stiffen as she started a very slow grind.

"I'll take my punishment now," Taija whispered on a seductive sigh.

Duron obliged her by first rubbing her belly where his baby was already growing and then proceeded to undress her.

"Speaking of secrets, are we ready to tell my family yet that you're pregnant? I see what Loren's secret did to me and I don't want to keep any secrets from my family."

Taija was about to respond when her mind drifted to how he was caressing her after he removed her dress.

"Taija, did you hear me?" Duron said as he continued to stroke her then kissed her ear, just the way she liked.

"Yes, but I'm busy taking my punishment like a bad girl."

No more talking was needed. Duron reached to untie the strings at her sides that held her strip of a thong in place and proceeded to punish her like only he could.

Chapter 17

Mike had just arrived home from being on the west coast for a week. He had a lot of work to catch up on and he also needed to talk to Duron. As bad as he also wanted to see Loren, he needed to clear the air with his best friend and make him understand that what he felt for Loren was unequivocal love. He headed straight for the condo where he knew he would run into Duron who would most likely be in the office.

As he suspected, when he got off of the elevator he could hear Duron on a business call so he headed for his office.

Duron noticed Mike standing in the doorway while he was on the phone and waved him in. Mike came into the office, shut the door and took a seat while Duron finished his call. He was determined to not leave the office until he and Duron had worked this out. They had been friends for too long to let anything come in between the two of them.

Duron ended his call, leaned back in his chair and looked over at Mike.

Mike spoke first.

"I love her Duron. She isn't a booty call or a play thing.

Like I told you in California, I love her and I have for a long time, but I fought that feeling because she was your sister and I wasn't sure how things would turn out. I am sorry that you walked in on us like that, but I'm not sorry for being with her. She makes everything in my world alright. I can talk to her about anything and it feels good just to be around her. I would do anything for her. I would give my life for her and I would never, ever hurt her. I know that's your biggest concern. If I had a sister and I was in your position, that would be my main concern, but trust me here, I love Loren. I am in love with Loren. I know you're pissed off with me, but we've been friends a long time; long enough for you to know that I would not have taken a step toward her if I were not genuine about my feelings for her. I hope we can get beyond this and if there is anything else that I could say or do that would reassure you that I am sincere in my feelings for her, I'm open to doing it. She's worth it," Mike exclaimed.

He watched as no emotion appeared on Duron's face. His face was a blank slate. He came here looking for a fight today with his best friend and at the moment he didn't know how to take his non-reaction.

Duron stared at Mike. He was not only listening to the words he was saying, but he was looking at his body language and the deep emotion on his face. He had no doubt at all that his friend was sincere. What he saw on Mike's face and heard in his every word was love for Loren and he could appreciate that.

"Mike, we're good. I'm serious man, we're good."

Duron saw a touch of relief on his friends face.

"I will tell you what I told my sister. I was surprised and caught off guard when I walked in your house. I wasn't expecting to see my sister. I wish you both hadn't kept it from me. She said that was her idea and I understand her reason for wanting to do so. I'm happy for you both and I can't fault either of you for finding the kind of love I've found with Taija. What kind of brother would I be if I couldn't be happy for my sister when she tells me she's in love."

Mike relaxed and sat back, comfortably in the chair. He had prepared for a fight and apparently he didn't need to.

"Are you sure you're okay with this? It's me, man. Tell me what you need from me to be sure we're okay?"

"You know what I need? I need you to not hurt my sister. You remember the basket case she was after her relationship with that Sam guy. I never want to see that look on my sister's face again. I want your guarantee that you won't hurt her."

"I won't hurt her. You have my word. I love her and I wouldn't do anything to hurt her."

Duron trusted Mike's words and just wanted to move forward.

"Good, that's all I need to hear. Now, since you're here can we talk some business? You don't have much longer before your move to California and we still have a lot to do. Speaking of the move, I don't want to keep getting all in the middle of your relationship with Loren, but how will this move affect the relationship and the work that needs to be done. California is a long ways away from Atlanta?"

Duron was right and he and Loren had talked about it and decided they would give the long distance relationship a try.

"As for Loren and I, we've decided to give it a try and make it work. As far as the work, we are very much on target. The contracts you and Tyrone signed before I left have been signed by me. I brought the checks back with me and we are ready to roll. I have a few weeks of working things out on this end in Atlanta and then I'm on my way. Thanks to Loren, all the rest of the furniture for the office and for my house should arrive over the next two weeks. Right now we are on schedule with everything. I would have come back sooner, but I had several furniture deliveries. Your sister really did a great job on my house. You and Taija will have to get to California soon to check it out."

Duron decided to tell his best friend about the baby since they had plans to tell the rest of the family this week.

"I'll be glad to come out and see it, but Taija won't be flying for a while. She's pregnant and the morning sickness has been hard on her. I'm not sure she's up to flying since riding in the car for a long period of time upsets her stomach. Can you believe I'm going to be a father?"

Mike got up to congratulate him.

"Congratulations on the baby. You two didn't waste any time I see."

"I know. Taija said she wanted kids right away and after talking about it, I realized I did also. We recently found out and she's been dealing with a bad case of morning sickness since then. We're telling the rest of the family this week."

"That's great news D. I know when Loren finds out she'll be over the moon with excitement."

"You're right about that. I know how she is with my niece and nephew and I'll have to talk to her about spoiling my kid. Let's head into the conference room for a few if you have the time. There's a big project that may be on the horizon that I want Tyrone to take the lead on. He and I have been talking about it and I want to bring you up to date with our thoughts."

"Yeah, I have time. I need to get unpacked and then I was planning to go see Loren. I'm sure she'll be happy to know that we worked things out. I know she has a lunch date with one of her assistants so I have some time until she's done. I can't wait to hear about a possible new project."

~~

Loren left her condo to meet with one of her assistants for a working lunch outside of the office. As she pulled out of her garage, putting on her dark shades to block the sun, she was about to make a left turn to head into downtown Atlanta when she swore she again saw the woman, Shelly, who Mike had been involved with. Now, Loren thought, the chick knew where she lived and was stalking her and not Mike. She was happy that there was no way Shelly could get into her building because the security was very tight. She didn't acknowledge that she saw Shelly. She continued to drive making a mental note to tell Mike about it later.

Loren actually felt sorry for Shelly. She knew where Shelly was coming from. She remembers when she first realized Sam was no longer hers, she would get a girlfriend or two of hers to go with her while she staked out places he would go to see who he was with. It wasn't healthy for her back then and it certainly wasn't healthy for Shelly now. She wishes there was something Mike could do to finally get her to leave them alone.

She continued on and when she reached the coffee shop where she was meeting her assistant, she found a parking spot and went in. She looked around and didn't see any more signs of Shelly. She shrugged it off, sat down and ordered a light lunch and waited.

She smiled when her cell phone rang, seeing her brother's number show up on the screen.

"Hey D," she said with a lot of excitement.

"Hey sis. Listen I wanted to tell you before you heard it from someone that I'm going to be a father in a little under seven months."

Loren almost fell out of her chair. This was great news.

"Wow D, you work fast," Loren responded smiling with glee.

"No kidding. Taija said she wanted to start a family right away. She's an only child and she wants to be sure we start early enough to have two or three."

"Congratulations, D. Have you told mom and dad yet?"

Loren knew her mother would be over the moon with excitement. She loved being a grandmother and couldn't wait until all of her children blessed her with grandchildren to fill the house up with on holidays.

"No, Taija and I will be telling them soon. We just finished telling her mother this morning and she was very excited. I wanted to be sure I told you because I'm sure mom will call you as soon as Taija and I leave and I wanted you to hear it from me."

"Thanks D. I'm very excited for you. I did think that Taija's face was a little chubby when I saw her the other day, but I didn't want to say anything. Women hate that, especially if pregnancy is not the cause."

"Don't worry about it. That was definitely the reason. She just wanted to be a little further along before she told anyone in the family, but she said she's ready. She's been suffering really bad from morning sickness and even now she's complaining because of the amount of weight she has already picked up. She has an appointment with her doctor next week about all of the weight gain and I'm sure he'll tell her its normal."

"I'll call her in a little while. I want to congratulate her myself."

Loren could not contain her excitement.

"I'm going to be spoiling that baby rotten!"

Duron laughed loud.

"You better have an extra bedroom set up because he or she will be spending a lot of time with you if you start with the spoiling like you did with Lyric and Milo."

Loren looked up to see her assistant entering the building.

"D, I have to go. I have a meeting that's about to start."

Duron looked at his phone mystified that she hung up on him before he had a chance to utter another word. He didn't get the chance to tell her about his other reason for calling her. He wanted her to know that he and Mike had worked things out and he was happy for them and their love.

After they went over plans for a new project that Tyrone would lead, they talked a little more about how they'd both fallen in love after being 'bachelors for life' for so long. Duron knew how happy he was and he was glad that Mike finally settled down and found someone. Now that he was over the initial shock of how he found out, he was glad the love of Mike's life was Loren.

Chapter 18

Mike had just arrived at his office building to do some work when the guard in the lobby told him that he had a visitor waiting for him. When Mike turned around, he was surprised to see Shelly sitting, waiting for him. When she saw him, she stood to approach him. He didn't like seeing her at his place of business and it was apparent his many talks with her about not being interested in what she had to offer still wasn't sinking in. Frustration filled his head and he didn't want a scene at his place of business, but he wasn't in the mood to deal with her. His only thought was on Loren and the fact that they were planning a night of relaxation at her condo when he finished at the office. He refused to let Shelly ruin his mood. He did, however, need to talk to her about sightings of her at Loren's condo and other places he and Loren frequented. As she walked toward him, he planned his words carefully.

"Mike, it's good to see you baby. I've missed you and I know you've missed me by now so I thought I'd stop by to say hello."

"Shelly, you shouldn't be here?" he said, agitated.

"I know, but I wanted to talk to you and see you. Like I said I missed you."

He didn't miss how seductive she was trying to sound, but he had no interest in anything she had to say or offer and he was already losing patience.

"What do you need to talk to me about?"

"I was wondering if maybe you'd like to get dinner tonight and talk."

She seemed unsteady and he was concerned. He was familiar with her strong, no holds barred personality, but now she seemed disturbed.

"Shelly, that's not a good idea. I already told you I'm seeing someone."

"You've always been seeing someone else since we first met. Why is this so different?"

He looked around and noticed the guard was trying hard to hear what they were talking about and he realized this was not a good place to talk to her.

"Shelly, follow me so that we can talk please."

He led her to the bank of elevators and decided to go up to the condo where they could have some privacy and just in case she got a little loud, no one would be disturbed. He knew Duron never came to his condo anymore and Tyrone was out of town at a car show, his favorite down time activity.

After the elevator reached the condo level, he opened the door to his condo and escorted Shelly inside. Once inside he immediately turned around to tell her once again and hopefully for the last time that any and everything between them was over.

"Shelly, this has got to stop. All of the following me and

Loren around has to stop. No more showing up at my place of business; no more anything. You agreed just as I did in the beginning that what we had was just casual sex with no promises of anything. I don't understand the problem now."

Shelly had her back to him so he couldn't see that she was untying her coat. When she turned around and opened it, she had nothing on underneath. He knew the situation had just gone from bad to worse.

"Are you trying to tell me you don't want a taste of this? Your girlfriend would never need to know. You know how we do and I don't see a reason why we need to stop simply because you found a new tart. I've been dealing with you and other women for years and that's never stopped us before."

Mike had to get her out of his condo. He had no idea she came to see him naked. He should have found it out of the ordinary that she would have on a coat, even a thin one, on a nice warm day.

"We're not doing this and you have to leave. Fasten your coat back up and leave. I know what we had in the past and back then I would have been receptive to this, but I don't know how many times I have to tell you I'm involved with someone and it's not casual. What you and I had was casual, but even that is now over. You need to understand that and move on."

He watched as Shelly left her coat open and pushed it back further by placing her hands on her bare hips.

"Mike, I know that's how it started, but you have to admit that we were beginning to develop something special and I want that back."

He had no idea what she was talking about.

"Something special? Shelly we never had anything special going on because it was just sex. We had some fun and now that's over. You knew the score when we started so this new attitude of yours is new and not welcomed. Fasten your coat and I'll walk you down and please don't contact me again."

He could see everything he was saying wasn't getting through as she continued to stand before him with her coat wide open. He watched as she removed her hands from her hips and used them to grip her breasts, trying to lure him in. He had no doubt he was in love with Loren because Shelly's display was having no effect on him.

"Mike, you have to admit it was some great sex. I went along with that casual thing until you were ready to be more serious. I figured if you were thinking of being more serious with anyone, it would be me. We were spending a lot of time together and I want that back. I don't mind that you're seeing this Loren person. In fact I'm even open to you inviting her to join us for some fun. We talked about adding to our fun and she's pretty enough that I'd be okay with it."

The conversation was not going as he had planned. He now knew how right Loren was. Shelly was indeed a woman scorned and she was covering it by playing the role of seductress. He could now see that he was the blame for Shelly's current state. Even though he was involved with her strictly for the hot sex, he knew that she was feeling more for him than just sex, but he ignored what he knew was happening. This new Shelly was a lot to deal with. He needed to handle her a little softer so he spoke to her in a calmer voice.

"Look, I'm sorry if you thought that something more

was going on between us. If I led you on in any way I'm sorry and I apologize for doing that. I am involved with someone else and like I said, it's not casual. It's the real thing and I'm in love with her."

Once he mentioned the word love all color left Shelly's face. She went from being seductive to being angry.

"I never had a problem with you seeing other women and I don't mind now either. I don't see why this means you and I can't continue what we had. You don't fall in love with women, you screw them for sport."

"I'm sorry if you thought there was more to what we had, but there wasn't. I'm in love with her and very happy. I can't see you anymore and I need you to respect that. Stop following me around and stop stalking Loren. She told me she's been seeing you at her place of business, at her home and when she's with me. You have to stop this now Shelly, it's not healthy. I will never get involved with you again. You need to move on," he told her.

He knew the moment her anger began to boil over and he knew he needed to get her out of his condo immediately. He reached for the door to escort her back out and into the elevator. Before he could get far, she let him have it.

"You are a bastard Mike," she shouted as she stepped out of his condo and walked toward the elevator, still with her coat wide open.

"Shelly cover yourself up."

She ignored him and once again opened the coat wider by placing her hands on her hips.

"You think you led me on? Well, yes you did. You men have no idea what it does to a woman to be played with. How dare you treat me like I was nothing to you. I know we were having fun, but I care about you. I fell in love with you and this is how you treat me because you found a new piece?"

Mike let her speak and she got louder and angrier with every word.

"I love you Mike and here you are telling me you love someone else."

"Love Shelly? We were having sex, not falling in love. What I have with Loren is real, true love. What we had was only sex. That has always been the case. It's not new and you know it. I understand you're hurt and I'm sorry about that."

"It was only sex to you Mike, but to me it was much more than that and you are a pathetic example of a man for leading me on the way you did. What about all the things you said to me?"

"Those are things said in the heat of passion Shelly. They weren't whispers of love. I never once said I loved you and I never led you to believe that we would have anything more than what we had."

He watched as her anger turned to uncontrollable rage.

"Rot in hell Mike," she said, spitting each word out with such venom, Mike could feel the hatred in each word she spoke.

She turned away from him, still not closing her coat and pushed the button, wiping her eyes at the same time.

"You know what they say about Karma Mike, so remember that."

Just then the elevator door opened and before Shelly could get in, Mike looked to see Loren standing in the elevator. His world just crashed and the Karma Shelly had just mentioned was visiting him with a vengeance. He didn't know what to say and he was glued to his spot at the door as he watched Loren try to evaluate the situation before her.

Loren couldn't move. The sight before her was a shock to her system.

She had come to Mike's condo to take him up on his offer to accompany her to her parent's house to talk to her mom and dad about their relationship. She originally told him she would do it by herself, but as she began driving to their house, she thought that she would be more effective if they did it together. She turned her car around and headed to his condo, knowing he was heading first to the office to get some work done and then to his condo to wait for her call about how her talk with her parents went. She had tried calling his cell and he never answered so she just showed up since she had a key that would let her off on the penthouse level.

She used her spare key to the corporate floors of the elevator to first check his office and when she didn't see him there, she got back in the elevator to catch up with him at home. What she didn't expect to see when she got to the condo was Mike standing in his doorway and Shelly look as if she was coming from his condo stark naked. Time stood still as she took in the scene, not sure what to make of it. Mike saw her and Shelly recognized her, but no one moved.

"Well look who we have here," Shelly said entering the elevator.

Mike was in trouble when he saw what first looked like confusion turn to hurt on Loren's face. Before he could get his feet to move, Shelly pushed the button to close the elevator door and turned and smiled at him, still with her hands on her naked hips.

Shelly thanked Karma.

"I appreciate the good time Mike," he heard her say before she once again gripped her breasts just as the elevator door closed with Shelly and Loren together on the inside.

Fear like nothing Mike had ever felt before overcame him. He tried pushing the button to get the elevator to return and open, but he realized he needed his key for that and he'd put it on the table when he walked into the condo followed by Shelly. He ran into his condo, grabbed his key and ran back to the elevator to see if he could get it to return. When he realized it wasn't working, he darted for the steps and decided to run down to catch the elevator. He knew luck wasn't on his side because Karma was in control, but he had to try. He had to know that Loren was okay and that Shelly wasn't filling her head with lies. Her last show of gripping her breasts and commenting on them having a good time was not what he wanted Loren to thin happened. He needed to get to her.

Shelly loved how this was turning out. She couldn't have planned this better if she'd tried to. This so called woman that Mike claimed he loved was in the elevator and she was sure her mind was going crazy wondering what had taken place. Since they were stuck together in the elevator she couldn't think of a better time to get her revenge on being tossed aside like trash.

She proceeded to slowly close and zip her coat over her nakedness.

"This thing with you and Mike won't last long. I hope you know that," Shelly said to Loren.

Loren noticed she spoke with a lot of attitude and anger.

"Don't believe that he is as into you as he says he is. He's told me the same lies I'm sure he's telling you. I bet he told you he loved you. He told me the same thing and as a matter of fact, right before he, you know reached his peak before rushing me out, he screamed he loved me and only me. It was exhilarating and hot and sexy. He loves when I show up naked and he was an animal. I'm guessing you're not satisfying him. If you had shown up a little earlier, we really could have had some fun. We have talked about adding a third and you are sexy enough that I'd go for it. Just don't think he's in love with you. Clearly he's not a one woman man."

Loren didn't respond. She didn't know what happened between them before she showed up, but it was clear something had and it felt like someone had stuck a knife in her heart and sliced it to pieces.

"Feel free to go back up and get you some. That man is a stallion, which I'm sure you know. I just want you to know that I'll be here waiting for him when he drops you like he has other women he was seeing while seeing me. I always end up on top."

Loren listened, but still didn't respond as Shelly spoke. She didn't want to upset her any more than she already was. She just wanted the elevator to hurry and get to the lobby so that she could get out. She was going to go home and connect with Mike later after the situation cooled off. She knew there had to be an explanation around what she saw. There was no way she was going to believe that what they shared was not real. She loved him and he loved her and she knew it. For now, she needed some space and she wanted to get as far away from this angry woman as she possibly could.

When the elevator reached the lobby, Shelly turned to Loren and said, "I'll be seeing you around. Enjoy your time with Mike while you can. I don't care how long you've been seeing each other, he belongs to me. Like I said, I'm not letting you or any other woman take him from me. Let's be very clear about that."

Loren, still never saying a word, watched the woman walk out of the elevator. She waited until the doors were about to close before she exited herself. She was going to head home, but decided she just needed a little air. She decided to walk a block or two to clear her head and to make sure that before she got in her car, she was focused.

Mike, exhausted from running down flights of stairs decided to try the elevator again when he reached the office level. To his luck, once he put his key in, he heard the elevator move and according to the lit up numbers, it was coming back up from the lobby. Maybe Loren was still in it he thought since he knew she would have parked in the garage and the elevator didn't appear to go down that far.

The elevator quickly reached his level and when the doors opened, his heart sank when he didn't see Loren. He got in and took the elevator to the lobby. The security guard told him that there were two ladies in the elevator and they both exited on the main lobby floor. Mike thanked him and ran out of the door looking to see what direction Loren went in because he needed to talk to her. He didn't know what Shelly had told her, but he was sure it was a lie. He knew that Loren was probably wondering what Shelly was doing coming out of the condo naked, especially when he knew Loren wasn't expected to be there. He needed to catch her and do it fast so that they could talk.

He wasn't sure how things had gotten out of control. He never took the time to notice how unstable Shelly was. It wasn't until his conversation today with her that the light bulb started to shine bright over the entire situation. He never meant to hurt her or lead her on. All along he thought they were both having fun when time permitted. He had no idea she had fallen in love with him and that love, not being returned had turned into a dangerous obsession. He felt bad and he wished he knew of a better way to handle the situation. He knew Loren would understand when he told her why he had taken Shelly up to the condo to talk which was so that they could have a little privacy to finally end things. He could only imagine the things that were going through Loren's mind when she saw them at his condo. All he needed to do was talk to her and let her know that she was right about Shelly being more into him than he was into her. He was sure he would be able to reassure Loren that nothing happened and that Shelly was unstable and it was his fault. He felt sorry for her, but he didn't know what else to do other than to tell her it was over and that he was in love with someone. Mike went in search of Loren, in the direction the security guard said she headed.

~ ~

Loren was walking and gathering her thoughts. She saw the hurt on Shelly's face and she heard the hurt in her voice no matter how much she tried to cover it with insinuations that she and Mike had just had wild sex. She had once been that same woman so she knew how she felt. She tried to warn Mike that he may have gotten the signs crossed with Shelly. She would walk a block or two to clear her head and then go back in to talk to Mike, when she was sure that Shelly was indeed gone.

She had walked almost two blocks when she decided to

turn around and head back to Mike's place. As she headed back in that direction, she saw Mike on the opposite side of the street, waiting for the light to change. She noticed the minute Mike spotted her. He looked agitated like he couldn't wait for the light to change. He waved at her so that she could see and wait for him. She went to wave back until she spotted Shelly in her car looking right at Mike. She was about a half block away from where she and Mike stood, sitting in her car, idling.

Loren could see clear enough that tears were pouring down Shelly's face and she could see the black lines of eyeliner as it ran down her face. All Loren could feel was fear. She had a feeling this was about to turn very bad. The way Shelly was looking at Mike spoke volumes and Loren needed to get his attention. She watched as Shelly gripped the steering wheel like a mad woman and when she sped in Mike's direction, Loren knew what was about to happen. She acted quickly and called Mike's name to warn him to step back up onto the curb.

Just as Mike heard Loren call his name and yelled for him to watch out, he turned his head in the direction that she was pointing in and made a split second decision to back up towards the curb just as Shelly veered toward him with her car. Everything that happened next seemed to happen in slow motion.

He watched helplessly as Shelly looked at him like a crazed woman and turned the direction of her car away from him and headed straight for Loren on the opposite side of the street. Before he could react, Shelly plowed into the crowd standing on the corner with Loren and again, in slow motion, he watched as the car sent everyone on that corner up in the air and down to the street like they were pins being hit by a bowling ball. In the midst of that crowd was Loren. Mike held his breath as he saw Loren laying in the street, her leg twisted at an awkward position, not moving. In all of the mayhem that started to take place, he darted across the street, the short distance to get to Loren, all the while his heart was beating faster and faster. He prayed that she was okay. As he reached her, he also grabbed his phone at the same time and dialed 911.

"911 operator, how can I help you?"

"Yes, my name is Michael Bailey and there's been an accident at the corner of Collier and Peachtree. There are several people here who have been hit by a car and some with serious injuries. We need an ambulance and the police please."

He tried to remain calm and not lose control. He needed to stay calm so that he could help Loren and the others.

"Sir, we have several people also reporting this accident and police and ambulance services are on the way."

Mike dropped his phone as he tried to tend to Loren who was not moving.

"Loren, baby, can you hear me? Don't move. Help is on the way. I love you baby, please be okay," he pleaded.

He felt a need to pick up her body and cradle her to him to protect her, but he didn't because he didn't know what injuries she had sustained besides the obvious one to her leg, He also noticed a huge gash on the side of her head and it was bleeding very heavily.

There was screaming and hollering from everyone in the crowd and he could barely hear the sound of the sirens coming to the scene of the accident. He continued to hold Loren's hand and whispered words of encouragement to her just in case she could hear him. He wanted her to know he was there with her and that he would not leave her. Mike knew in his heart he would never, ever leave her as he silently played for God to spare her life. He didn't know what he would do without her. He continued to pray until a medic from one of the ambulances asked him to step aside so that he could tend to Loren to assess her injuries. He didn't want to step away or leave her side, not even for a minute, but he knew he had to so that they could work to save her life.

'God please let her be okay,' Mike said to himself over and over.

While the medics worked feverishly on Loren and the others who were hit, he looked to where Shelly's car had come to a rest after hitting a pole. She was being pulled from the car by the police. As she was pulled out, she looked right at him, with her tear stained face and simply said, "I'm sorry."

He didn't care if she was sorry or not. All he knew was she had turned his world upside down by her senseless act. No amount of saying she was sorry could ever fix what she had caused. In her anger and hatred, she had run down a dozen people, not caring about anyone's life. He watched as she was placed in a police car and then they headed in his direction. He again looked down as the medics spoke to hospital personnel to let them know the state of Loren's condition.

Hearing that Loren was unconscious, critical but stable, Mike knew he needed to contact her family. He watched as the medics prepared Loren for transport to the hospital.

"Can you tell me which hospital she's being taken too? I want to call her family."

"We're taking them all to Atlanta Medical Center."

Mike knew that was the hospital where Loren's father was chief of surgery and her brother Jake was also a physician.

"Can you get word to the hospital that this is Loren Knight? Her father is Earl Knight, chief of surgery and her brother Jake is also a doctor there. They should know that she's coming in as a patient."

"Yes sir, we will do that," the medic replied and made that announcement to the dispatcher.

Mike thanked him, reached for his phone and dialed Duron. He answered on the second ring and began talking before Mike could get a word in.

"Hey bro, I was just about to call you. Taija and I want to have you and Loren over for dinner sometime next week if...."

Mike cut him off.

"D, man, listen. There's been an accident. I'm down the street from the office and Loren was hit by a car."

"What!!!!" he heard Duron shout.

"Actually it was Shelly who hit her. She was gunning her car to hit me when Loren screamed for me to watch out. When she did, Shelly turned the car towards Loren and hit her and a group of other people standing on the opposite side of the street."

He could hear Duron moving around, probably heading out of the office faster than speedy Gonzales from the cartoons.

"How bad is she Mike? I'm on my way down right now."

"She's pretty bad. She's unconscious and I heard the medic say she was critical, but stable. They're about to transport her to the hospital right now. I also had them alert your dad and brother that they were bringing her in so that they could meet the ambulance. D, I'm going to go with her to the hospital in the ambulance. Take a breath for a second bro. They are taking her where your brother and father work so she will get the best immediate care. I think you need to call your brother Brian and probably get to your mom's house and pick her up."

Duron knew he was right. His father and brother would take care of Loren and Mike would be there with her also. He needed to get to his mother before she heard about it either while watching the news or from someone who may have recognized Loren and called the house.

"You're right. She's at home and Taija is with her. I'm heading there now and I'll pick them up and meet you at the hospital. Make sure you call me with any updates or if anything changes."

"Gotcha bro. I'm not leaving her side. I love her."

"I know you do. I'll see you in a few," Duron said before hanging up.

Chapter 19

Mike paced back and forth in the emergency room waiting for any word on Loren's condition. As he paced, he noticed her brother, Brian racing down the hallway followed by Taija and Duron who was guiding his mother who looked as if she were on unsteady legs. He knew they were all anxious to hear how Loren was doing.

"Mike, what's the latest? Where are my dad and Jake?"

"They're still with her in emergency. They haven't come out yet. Your dad told one of the nurses to let him know when you arrived. I just told her you were here so she's letting him know."

"What the hell happened Mike? You said Shelly hit her on purpose with her car? Why? What was going on?"

Mike could see the anger brewing up in Duron and he didn't blame him. This was all his fault. He put Loren in danger by exposing his relationship with Loren to Shelly. He sent Shelly over the edge by declaring his love for Loren. Shelly took that anger and hurt the woman he loved and he would never forgive himself for it. He started to explain when Duron's mother interjected.

"Not now boys."

She then turned to Duron.

"You need to calm down. I can see how angry you are and right now is not the time for anything other than praying for your sister and all of the others who were hurt. I don't want to hear anything else right now besides prayer," she said sternly.

Duron and Mike looked from each other to Duron's mother and nodded their agreement. She was right. Mike would give them the entire story later. Right now, they needed to pray that Loren was alright. They were about to join hands and pray when the emergency door opened and Loren's father and brother came through followed by two other doctors.

Mike watched as Mr. Earl, Loren's dad, went straight for his wife, embracing her and telling her everything was going to be alright. Everyone held their breath, nervous about Loren's condition. Her brother Jake spoke first.

"Loren is critical. There was major trauma to her body. This is Doctor Draper and Doctor Morgan. They are Loren's doctors and will be sure that Loren gets the best care. They are about to have her sent down for some tests, x-rays, the whole trauma care rundown so that we can be sure of all of Loren's injuries. For now she's stable, but she is very critical. Doctor Morgan will give the update."

"Thanks Dr. Knight," Dr. Morgan said. "She has very obvious leg injuries and we know that her left leg is broken in two places. She also has a fractured left arm. She has some head trauma as well. We're sending her for scans to determine the extent of the head trauma. As soon as we have test results, we'll come back out to give you all an update."

Jake thanked them both as they headed off to tend to Loren. He once again spoke to the family.

"Dad and I are going to step back to allow everyone to do the best job for Loren and we're going to be here with you as family, waiting. Let's all have a seat. Duron, get mom some water and get her seated. She doesn't look too steady."

Mike watched as Mr. Earl tended to his wife, making sure she was okay. She was near hysterics and they all wanted to keep her calm.

"Jake, go get your mother something to calm her down," Mr. Earl said. "I don't like how upset she is. We need to get her calmed."

Jake headed in a sprint to follow his dad's instructions. Mr. Earl hollered at Jake's back, "Jake, bring back a blood pressure cuff."

Jake nodded his understanding.

Mike watched from a short distance as Loren's family catered to her mother. He was also concerned as he saw that she was having a hard time catching her breath, being upset at the news of Loren's injuries. He looked around at the scene, knowing this was all his fault and he silently prayed that the woman he loved more than anything would be okay.

Two police officers approached Mike while he was waiting with the family on the status of Loren's condition.

"Sir, are you Michael Bailey?"

Mike, stood, acknowledging their question.

"Yes I am."

"I'm Officer Jackson and this is office McMillan. We were wondering if we could ask you some questions about the accident today. Your name was given to us as a witness to what happened and we were told that we would be able to reach you here at the hospital."

"Sure," Mike replied. "I gave one of the officers on the scene my information so that someone could follow-up later. What can I answer for you?"

The officers both looked from Mike to Loren's family who were listening to the conversation. Mike could see that the officers were wondering if they should speak in front of everyone.

"Should we go someplace private?" one of the officers asked.

"No it's fine talking in front of everyone. This is the family of one of the people hit by the car today. They are like family to me."

"Fine sir. Can you tell us what you know and what you saw occur today?"

"I can give you a lot of insight into what happened. I'm going to start with telling you the precursor to the accident. The woman driving the car that hit all those people standing on the corner is a woman I have a history with. Prior to the accident we had a conversation that had gotten pretty heated and she was very upset. She stormed away after our conversation and as I was about to cross the street, Loren, one of the people hurt, called out to me to look out. I looked in the direction that Loren was pointing and saw Shelly, the driver, gun her car and aim it towards me. I moved back out of the street and as she got closer, she turned her car away from me and towards Loren and just plowed into them."

"Thank you for that information sir. You said she, the driver, deliberately drove into the crowd of people standing on the corner?"

"Yes sir. She never let up on the gas. She did a hard turn to the left and went deliberately into them. It may have been that she was going after Loren. She was upset after just learning that my relationship with Loren was pretty serious and she was very upset about that."

"We were able to speak with the driver and she did say she did it on purpose and it was a bad spur of the moment, rash decision and that she was sorry. She didn't mean for any of this to happen."

Mike wanted to know what would happen to Shelly. He was upset at what she did, but he didn't wish her any ill will.

"Officer, do you know what will happen to the driver?"

"Once we are able to get information from all of the witnesses, I'm sure some charges will be filed against her."

One of the officers dug out a business card and handed it to Mike.

"I'm sure we will want to speak to you again. For now, if you have any questions here is my information. Can we get your phone number and address for the report and in case we have additional questions for you?"

Mike reached for his wallet to retrieve one of his business cards.

"My contact information is on the front. I'll write my home address and home phone number on the back for you."

After doing so, the officers thanked Mike for his time and headed off to talk to others in the hospital waiting area who may have been witnesses as well.

Mike turned back to the family and wondered if they thought badly of him. He was wondering if they were thinking that his womanizing ways had finally come back to haunt him, haunt them all. Looking at them, they didn't appear to be holding any type of anger or grudge against him. They were their normal, loving selves.

As they all waited, Duron came up to Mike to check on him.

"Hey man, you good?" Duron asked.

"Yeah, I am. Just worried like hell about Loren. I can't believe all this has happened. Why didn't I recognize Shelly was unstable before it got to this point?"

"Mike, man don't do this to yourself. You can't take responsibility for what she did. I know you man and I know you were clear with her from the start about the type of relationship you two were going to have and I know you wouldn't lead her on while seeing Loren as well. There was no way for you to know how she would react. Only Shelly would know that."

Mike shook his head, understanding where Duron was coming from.

"That same love bug that bit you, bit me when it came to your sister. She is unlike any woman I have ever been involved with. She completes me and I never want to imagine life without her. I love her very much. Who would have thought that I would ever be ready to say those words to anyone," Mike declared.

Duron knew exactly how Mike felt. He felt the same way every time he looked at his wife. She was his life and he would never stand in the way of Loren and Mike having the kind of happiness that he and Taija shared.

"Loren is going to be fine Mike. You'll be able to tell her how much you love her every day."

Duron patted Mike on the back to reassure him and went to check on his mother.

Mike was the first to see Dr. Morgan come through the emergency room doors.

"Hello everyone. I have a private room where I'd like to speak with the family in, instead of this open space. Follow me please."

Mike stood still. He was afraid of the news the doctor would have to share, especially when he carted them off to a private room. This was all his fault and he didn't feel worthy to join the family. He didn't know how he would look Loren's mother in the face again if the doctor came in with very bad news.

It was Loren's mother that first noticed that Mike didn't follow behind them.

"You all go and walk ahead. I'll be right along," Ms. Barbara said while looking over at Mike. Everyone knew the kindness in Ms. Barbara's heart would not allow her to leave Mike sitting there alone feeling like this was all his fault and feeling like he was no longer a part of the family. To her he was a son and she needed to reassure him as any mother would reassure any of her children.

She turned from the family and walked over to Mike.

Mike looked up at Ms. Barbara with unshed tears in his eyes. He could see the worry in her face and was sorry that he was the cause of it. Before she could say anything he needed to apologize.

"I'm so sorry Ms. Barbara. I never meant for any of this to happen. I didn't realize how out of control Shelly was. I didn't pay attention to how unstable she was."

"Michael, do you love my Loren?"

"I love her more than life itself, Ms. Barbara. She is everything in this world to me."

"I didn't know you two were seeing each other, but now

that I know, I want you to understand that this was not your fault and you are still just as much a part of this family as you always have been. I know you didn't cause this. You could not have. You would never do anything to intentionally hurt Loren. I don't even believe you set out to intentionally hurt that young lady who hit Loren with her car either. Right now all that matters is that you love Loren and right now she needs you with her. Get up from that seat and follow me into this room. Every time they ask for the family, you stand your ground and stay close. I have known for a very long time that Loren loved you. I'm just glad that the day came when the two of you found out how you felt about each other. Don't push away now thinking you don't belong. She is going to want to see you when she wakes up. I don't know all that has been going on between you two, but I know that Loren would want you with us, so come on. Let's go hear what we need to do to help Loren come through this. I have faith that God is watching over her and I'll continue to pray for covering and I want you to do the same thing and I want you to do it while standing with this family; your family. I don't want you taking the blame for this or feeling down about it. You stay strong because Loren is going to need you."

Mike got up and followed her into the room to hear the latest on Loren's condition.

Dr. Morgan began just as they entered the room.

"Let me first say that Loren is going to be fine. We did a CT scan and could see that Loren has some swelling around the brain that we can treat with medication, so no surgery will be needed for that. We will continue to watch that. Most of the damage to her head is surface cuts and lacerations and those are being taken care of now. Due to the swelling, Loren has not woken up yet and that's a good thing. We're going to leave her as critical, but stable to be sure she is watched non-stop around the clock. Our biggest concern is reducing the swelling around her brain and again we are on top of that. We have set the leg and her arm in casts and we're keeping them elevated to help with the blood flow. I'm going to let Dr. Draper give you an update on the baby."

Together, everyone in the room except the doctors said, "Baby?"

"What baby?" Duron said.

The doctors looked at the family and realized no one knew that Loren was pregnant.

"I'm sorry. I thought you all knew that Loren was pregnant."

All eyes turned to Mike who stood with a look of shock on his face, speechless. He wasn't quite sure he heard the doctor correctly and needed to be sure.

"I'm sorry, did you say Loren is pregnant?" he asked. He noticed all eyes in the room were still on him.

"Yes, Loren is about four weeks along, very early in the pregnancy," Dr. Draper confirmed. "It's why Dr. Morgan called me in to assist. With trauma cases, before we do any work on them or administer any medication, we like to be sure of any pregnancy and since Loren was unconscious, we quickly did a blood test and determined she was indeed pregnant so that we could plan our strategy for saving not only Loren, but the baby as well. We are pretty confident the baby is fine so please don't worry."

Everyone continued to stare at Mike who wanted to assure them that he didn't know. He spoke to the entire family, but looked at Ms. Barbara when he spoke.

"I had no idea Loren was pregnant. She didn't say anything to me."

Everyone looked around the room to see if anyone appeared to have known. They all then looked at Taija who also confirmed that Loren did not tell her either.

Dr. Draper broke the silent stares.

"It's very possible Loren didn't know yet. Either way, yes she's pregnant and the baby is fine. I will be keeping a close eye on the baby and have listed the restrictions on medication in her chart so that nothing is administered that could harm the baby."

Dr. Morgan continued with an additional update.

"The biggest impact Loren took from the accident was to her leg, arm and the head injury was a result of the fall she took after being hit. From what I'm told there were two other people who took the brunt of the hit from the car and who sustained more serious injuries and a lot of what Loren could have taken was blocked by her being more behind those two people. Everyone from the accident will be fine. There were lots of broken bones, but thank goodness there was no loss of life."

Everyone was relieved to hear that and they were especially elated to hear that Loren would be okay.

"Once the swelling on Loren's brain has reduced, she should wake up and we can do a better job of assessing any type of brain damage. We don't believe there is any significant damage, but of course we want to be absolutely sure. We will cross that road when we get to it. Right now, we will continue to monitor her progress. You can go in to see her in a few minutes; no more than two people at a time."

Everyone listened as the doctor continued with more

instructions, especially on what they should be prepared to see.

"Be ready for what you see when you walk into the room. There is a lot of bruising, especially on her face. That will go down. We are doing everything for Loren and if you have any questions at any time, please don't hesitate to have one of the nurses page me. I will continue to give you updates and I have assured both Dr. Knight's that I will closely monitor Loren's progress to keep you all updated around the clock. I would say that Loren could wake up at any time and we don't see any prolonged damage to her not waking up. It's just a matter of time and if I can do anything else for any of you, please let me know."

Loren's father thanked both doctors for the update then walked out with them and Jake. That left everyone else thankful for the news that Loren would be okay and stunned by the fact that Loren was pregnant.

Mike sat down in the nearest chair, overwhelmed by the news that he was going to be a father.

"My baby is having a baby? Well isn't this some revelation. Thank God she's going to be alright and that the baby is fine too," Ms. Barbara said.

Mike continued to be in a daze at the news. Loren was pregnant with his child and he was going to be a father. He wondered if she knew when she stopped in to see him at the condo earlier when she ran into Shelly leaving. He wondered if she was coming to tell him about the baby. He was happy about the baby, but he was even more ecstatic that Loren was going to pull through okay. She was still in some danger due to the head injury, but he had faith that she would pull through okay with that as well.

"I need to see my baby," Ms. Barbara said. "I just need

to lay my hands on her so that I know she's okay."

"Okay, mom, come on. I'll go in to see her with you," Duron said. He turned to his wife before leaving.

"Taija, baby, are you okay? Maybe you should sit down. You look a little pale yourself," he said.

"I'm fine Duron. You go ahead. I just needed to sit down. I know it's not morning, but this baby has no sense of time," she replied.

"I'll have a nurse bring you some soda and crackers. Mike, Brian, look after her while I'm gone," Duron said before walking out with his mother.

"I got you bro. I'll go get her soda and crackers. You go ahead and take mom in to see Loren," Brian said before leaving the room.

After everyone had left, Mike and Taija were in the room alone, both taking in all that had transpired.

"I'm glad Loren is going to be okay," Taija said.

"I'm definitely breathing better hearing that she'll be okay. I wouldn't be able to handle it if anything had happened to her. I need her to be okay. She is everything to me and I mean everything. I never thought I would love anyone as much as I love her. I've dated a lot of women, but none have ever meant as much to me as Loren does."

"You know she loves you too, Mike. I still remember back in our college days when I would tease her about the crush she had on you. It didn't mean that much back then, but now I see that she meant it back then just as much as she means it now. You and Loren were meant to be. That baby she's carrying is a symbol of the love you two share. Congratulations on the baby."

"I just love her so much Taija. Yesterday, I went to the jewelry store and bought an engagement ring. I was planning to ask her to marry me today. She was going to tell her parents about us today and I was going to contact her father later to ask his permission to marry her. I still have the ring in my pocket. Today just went so wrong."

"I know Mike, but you can't blame yourself."

"I hear you, but that doesn't lessen the burden I feel for this situation. Shelly showing up at the condo today, right before Loren got there was poor timing. I didn't get a chance to explain to Loren what was going on with Shelly being at my place. I had invited her up to talk because I didn't want her making a scene in the lobby. I couldn't tell by Loren's facial expression if she was angry when she saw Shelly there. I felt sick when Shelly ran her car into that crowd. I still feel sick."

Taija got up to console Mike who was clearly shaken up by the events.

"Mike, there was no way for you to predict what Shelly would do. Loren shouted for you to look out because she loves you and didn't want to see you hurt. You couldn't know what Shelly was planning to do. I'm just hoping Shelly gets the help she needs. The police officer said that Shelly said she just snapped. All she could think of when she was in her car was the anger at knowing that she could never get you to fall in love with her and that she knew how much you loved Loren and she just didn't want anyone to have you."

"You're right. I'm hoping she gets the help she needs as well. I never, ever led her on, but I also didn't take notice of how deep her feelings were for me," he said.

Duron and his mother came back into the room where Mike and Taija were waiting.

"Mike, go ahead and see Loren. Go out this door, make

a right and she in the glass room at the end on the right."

Mike, nodded and went to visit the love of his life.

He entered her room and his heart took a nose dive when he saw her laying in the bed helpless. The doctors were right, she had a lot of swelling. He walked over to her and kissed her just in case she knew he was in the room.

"Loren, baby, I'm here. I'm right here and I'm not going anywhere. I need you to get better. I need you and our baby needs you. I'm sorry about all of this," he whispered.

He pulled a chair close to the bed, sat down, grabbed the hand that wasn't in a cast and prayed.

Chapter 20

Loren had been in the hospital for two days and in that time Mike only left briefly to run home to shower and to pick his mother up at the airport. When he called to tell her what happened to Loren, she could hear the hurt and loneliness in his voice and immediately booked a flight to be with him. He loved his mother and since she was his only child, he always got all of her attention. She loved hearing that he was in love and he knew that she was appreciative of how her family had always considered him a part of them since he and Duron had first become friends.

His father had died when he was a young boy and though his mother could never replace his father, she made sure he always felt loved.

After returning to the hospital with his mother in tow, Loren's mother decided to take a break from sitting in Loren's room and went with Mike's mother to the hospital cafeteria to get something to eat. He couldn't eat because he was too about Loren. He was thankful that the hospital had let him stay in the room with her beyond the normal fifteen minutes allowed with patients in intensive care. He wanted to be by her side as much as possible, just in case she woke up. He talked to her non-stop just in case she could hear him. He needed her to know that he was here, he loved her and would not leave her.

"Loren, it's day two baby and you still haven't woken up."

Mike slid his chair closer to the bed so that he could sit while still holding her hand. He wanted her to feel his warmth.

"I love you baby. I love you so much. I need you to wake up though. We have a baby that's two days older than when you first got here and we both need you. Did I mention that I hope the baby is a girl. I want her to be as beautiful inside and out just like her mommy is. Even with these bruises on your face, you are still the most beautiful woman in the world."

He stroked her cheek and her skin felt warm under this touch. He wanted her to wake up so that they could start their life together. He continued talking to her, hoping that she was able to hear everything he was saying. He looked from her face, down to her stomach where their child was growing inside of her. He was excited that in just short of eight months, he was going to be father. The news was unexpected, but welcomed. He leaned down and decided to have a conversation with his soon to be son or daughter.

He laid his head down on Loren stomach to talk directly to the baby growing there.

"Hey in there, it's your daddy. I'm glad you're going to be okay. Before yesterday, I didn't even know you were in there, but I'm glad I know today. I can't wait to meet you. You just continue to stay healthy and stay in there. You still have a long way to go before it's time for you to make your arrival and as much as we are all looking forward to meeting you, we want you to stay in your mommy's tummy until it's time for you to come out, so no early appearances because it's way too soon. Now, I want you to get use to my voice because you're going to be hearing it a lot. This is your daddy and I love you and I love your mommy very, very much."

As Mike leaned over to place a soft kiss on Loren's stomach, he felt her hand in his hair moving.

"Mommy loves daddy very much too," she whispered.

Mike raised up slowly to be sure he didn't startle her. Her eyes were still closed, but she was awake. He leaned closer to her face.

"Hi baby. I love you."

Loren slowly opened her eyes and looked right into his eyes.

"I love you too. I love you so much."

He leaned down and placed a soft kiss on her lips, ecstatic that she was awake. He needed to get the doctor.

"Baby, I'm coming right back. I'm going to go let everyone know that you're awake and get the doctor in here. We have all been waiting for you to wake up."

Before leaving the room, he placed a few soft kisses around her face.

"I'm glad you're back baby. You had us all so worried."

He turned to leave the room when he heard Loren say his name. Going back to the bed, he waited to hear what she needed.

"I'm here baby," he said.

"Mike, is the baby okay? Please tell me the baby is okay?"

Loren started to cry and Mike didn't want that. He knew she needed to remain calm.

"Loren, the baby is fine. The doctor said there was no damage done to the baby and it's still healthy. The baby is just fine so don't worry."

Loren just nodded and closed her eyes.

~~

Loren was more than ready to go home after being in the hospital over a week. Her doctors said she was coming along wonderfully with her recovery. The swelling had gone down and the bruising on her face was even clearing up. Her leg was still in its cast and it would be for a few more weeks. She was happiest knowing that the baby would be fine.

This wasn't exactly the circumstance by which she wanted Mike to find out that he was going to be a father, but she was glad he did know and that he was just as happy about the baby as she was when she first discovered she was pregnant. She was totally shocked when she took a home pregnancy test after missing her period.

Once her doctor had confirmed only a few days ago, she was overjoyed with the news of her baby's impending birth. She was more shocked knowing that they had always used condoms, but of course, even those are not one hundred percent effective.

She was happy to wake up to Mike in her room every day. He had been with her the entire week at the hospital, barely leaving her side. Her family and his mother had to threaten him with bodily harm in order to get him to leave to change clothes and to eat. He did pacify them as far as changing, but most of his meals he ate with her, in her hospital room. She smiled at the thought that he was at this very moment on his way to get her some chocolate, her favorite treat. The doctor finally said it was okay for her to have something other than hospital food and she wasn't sure if it was the baby or just the awful hospital food, but she craved chocolate like never before. She was thinking about how badly she wanted something chocolate when her parents entered the room after knocking to announce their presence.

"Hey baby girl!" her father said as they entered the room.

"Hi dad, hi mom."

"How are you feeling today?" her mother asked.

"Like I want to go home."

"I know dear, but not until the doctor gives the all clear."

"I know mom and I won't push it. I just miss my own bed and my own food. Dad, I don't know how you eat this hospital food every day. I need something fried and smothered in gravy!"

They laughed at pint sized Loren who ate everything in sight and never gained an ounce.

"For now Loren, just go with it and do exactly what Dr. Morgan says. You'll be out of here in no time."

There was silence before Loren's mother brought up the subject of the baby. They had not talked about the fact that she was pregnant all week because they wanted to be sure she was getting her strength up.

"So you and Mike are going to be parents, huh? Congratulations baby. I know we haven't talked about it, but if you're happy, we are happy for you."

"Yes, I'm very happy mom. I have to admit, I was shocked. It wasn't planned of course, but I'm just as happy as if it had been planned. I never really thought much about having children. Of course I always thought I'd be married first, but married or not, I can't wait to meet him or her."

"I'm excited too, Loren. You know how much I love Lyric and Milo. I love being a grandmother and there is something extra special when that grandchild is from a daughter. I will love all of my grandchildren the same, but there is something very, very special when your daughter is having a baby. I already know Michael is excited. You should have seen him the day the doctor revealed to us that you were pregnant. I thought he was going to pass out," her mother said and laughed.

Loren's dad could see that they were going to have an extensive conversation about the baby so he decided to give them some privacy and go check on some hospital business.

"I came by to check on you, but I'm going to go and get some work done. I'll be by later to check on you again before I go home."

After he left, she watched as her mother pulled a chair closer to the bed so that they could really talk.

"Why did you keep your relationship with Michael a secret for so long? Normally you can tell me anything. What happened that made you think you couldn't share this with me?"

Loren felt bad realizing the impact the secret has had on everyone.

"Mom, I'm sorry. I didn't really want to keep it from you at all. You know I like to tell you everything. I was planning to tell you the day of the accident. I wasn't expecting to fall in love with Mike. I thought that he and I would just keep it between the two of us, at least for a while. That while turned out to be longer than I thought and it was because I still wanted to keep it a secret. Mike was ready to tell everyone from the start. I didn't want there to be any animosity between him and Duron. I thought it would come and go and we would have had our time and it would be over with. It didn't happen that way. I didn't do it to distance the family. Duron recently found out about Mike and me and when they were able to talk through it, it was okay. I didn't find out about the baby until a few days before the accident. Mike and I were planning to have dinner later that night and I was going to tell him then. I wanted to tell Mike first and well you see how that turned out. Everything just turned so wrong. I'm so sorry for keeping my relationship from you. I didn't know how everyone would feel about us being together."

"Loren, I love Michael as if he was one of my sons. I think he is good for you and I think you make a perfect couple. I love you and as long as you are happy, I am happy."

Loren began to cry. She was blessed to have a mother as caring as she was.

"Thank you mom. I love him very much. He's my universe."

"I know baby girl. I can see that he feels the same way. You get some reset. I'll be back in a little later. I'm going to let others come in to visit with you."

Mike returned to Loren's room with chocolate in hand just as her mother was preparing to leave for the evening.

"Michael, don't you give the hospital staff trouble tonight with you trying to stay too late. Remember they have rules for a reason."

Mike nodded and accepted her hug.

"Bye mom. See you tomorrow."

"I see my knight in shining blue jeans and pull-over sweater has arrived with some chocolate."

"I have been waiting on this all day long. Apparently your child is a chocolate lover," Loren said as she shoved one piece of candy after the other in her mouth.

"So I assume, everything you eat during this pregnancy will be blamed on the baby?" he said as he laughed and sat on the bed next to her.

"Pregnant women can eat whatever they want and no one can say anything about it," she replied.

"You will get no argument out of me. I will get you anything you want. So Ms. Knight, I've been told to not give anyone a hassle about staying longer than I should tonight so I'm not going to stay long. I do want to talk before I leave."

He turned so that he and Loren were face to face.

"I'm sorry for all of this."

He saw Loren try to interrupt him, but he cut her off.

"Wait before you speak and interrupt me. I'm so sorry that all of this has happened. It doesn't matter how much everyone tells me that this is not my fault, I know that it is. I know I told you some of my dating history and a little about Shelly, but I want to explain more. Let me do that without interrupting, okay?"

Loren just nodded her agreement.

"Thank you. I met Shelly a few years ago and we had a friends with benefits situation going on, something I did tell you about. We always knew the score and we were both in full agreement. We saw each other when we had time and we made no promises. We were able to see other people and again, neither of us had an issue with that. I decided before we started our affair that I wasn't going to continue anything with her and I did let her know that and I told you I had no interest in any other woman and I didn't. I promise you nothing happened with Shelly and I after you and I slept together and I know how bad things looked in the elevator, but nothing happened. I wouldn't do that to you and I hope you believe that."

"Of course I do. I was shocked, but I didn't believe for one minute that you'd slept with her even though she insinuated that you did on the elevator ride down. I could see that she was upset and embarrassed and she wanted to hurt you and me."

"I'm glad to know you still have faith in my love for you. What I didn't take into consideration with all of this is that Shelly may not have been okay with me walking away. I believe she felt that if I were to ever decide that I was ready to commit to someone and settle down that it would be with her. When that didn't happen, her feelings for me overwhelmed her mental faculties and she snapped. She didn't want to believe that I was in love with someone that wasn't her. I never took her feelings for me serious even though the signs were there. I ignored them and did what a player would do. I brushed it off as something she would get over and she didn't. I didn't handle things well with her and because I didn't the end result was a lot of people being hurt by a woman with serious mental issues. For that I am sorry."

He paused as he carefully thought of his next words. They were words he hoped Loren was listening very closely to.

"I love you Loren. I know I've said it to you before and I know you know that I mean it every single time. Today I need you to understand exactly what my love for you means. It means that since the moment I first kissed you, there was never going to be another woman for me. You are my everything. I never, ever want to be without you. I want to marry you and make you my wife. I'm not saying this because of the baby. I had decided this days before any of this happened. I was planning to propose to you the same night that all of this happened, but things didn't quite turn out like I planned. Shelly was there only because she would have made a scene in the lobby and I needed to talk to her to get her to understand that things were completely over between she and I. I had no idea she was naked under that coat until she walked into the condo. I think I pushed her over the edge by my speech of how much in love with you I was and that there was no hope for she and I, ever. I hit her with it pretty hard because I was angry that she wouldn't just go away. I was meaner to her than I needed to be and I'm sorry for that because, yes it led to this."

He pointed to her leg as an example of what he was speaking of.

"In the beginning when we first started our affair, I was willing to go along with keeping it a secret as long as we could continue to see each other. I didn't want to let you go then and I'm not willing to go on without you and that would be the situation with or without the baby. I want to wake up each morning with you beside me and go to bed every night with you snuggled up in my arms the way you like to do when we spend the night together. I want to not only have this baby with you, but as many more as you would like to give me. You are the air that I breathe. I wake up each day and all is well with the world because you are a part of it with me. I know who I used to be and I don't want to be that lost soul anymore, going from woman to woman trying to find happiness without commitment. I'm ready to commit my everything to you and I hope you are willing to do the same thing because I would be miserable without you in my life permanently."

Loren didn't say a word because she was overwhelmed by the love she felt for him. This moment couldn't be more perfect. She knew that she had no plans of ever being without him again because she felt just as he did. Baby or no baby, they were meant to be together. She could feel the tears as they started to stream down her face at the thought of how much Mike really loved her and the feeling was mutual. She watched as he struggled to get something out of his pocket and her breath caught in her throat when he retrieved a blue velvet ring box from his pocket. As much as she wanted to say something, the words would not come. She thought that if she opened her mouth, she would really start bawling so she remained quiet and looked from the ring box he was now holding in his hand up to his eyes which were piercing her soul.

"Loren, baby, I love you more than anything in this world. Would you do me the honor of saying yes to being my wife and make me the luckiest man in the world? I promise to always honor you and our life together. I promise to always put you and our kids before anything else and I will devote my life to being the best husband, father, lover and friend you could ever ask for. You just have to say yes and I guarantee you will never regret that you did. I'm asking you today, will you be mine?"

He waited for what seemed an eternity while Loren took in the entire scene as he opened the ring box and showed her the marquee cute, platinum diamond engagement ring. He could see the glitter from the ring as it sparked in her eyes, full with tears. He was going to wait as long as she needed to gather her thoughts and words together.

Loren saw the ring and saw how absolutely beautiful it was. It wasn't the ring that drew her in. It was the look on the face of the man who stole her heart years ago and who was here today finally giving his to her and she wanted it without a doubt.

"Mike, I love you so much. Yes, I will be your wife today and every day. I can't wait to spend the rest of our lives together. I never, once, doubted your devotion to me."

She wanted to be sure he understood what she was about to say, so she reached out and placed her hands on both sides of his face and pulled his face right up to hers so that all of her words were very clear.

"I want you to know something so that we never have to talk about this again. You are not responsible for the reaction Shelly had to your conversation. You can't take the blame for her deciding to snap and hurt people by using her car as a weapon. She had a choice and she didn't choose right. I want to get this out in the open so that it does not continue to haunt our life together. I want you to let it go. Let the authorities do what they do and they will make sure Shelly gets the help she needs. You are a kind man with a big heart and you did not set out to hurt her. She couldn't handle letting you go because she knows you are a wonderful man, just as I know. I'm thankful that you chose me and I love you for that. We are going to have a wonderful life together as husband and wife. We will continue to pray for good health for Shelly, but we are moving on with our life and leaving all of this behind. Agreed?"

Mike nodded and took the opportunity afforded him at

the moment, being close to her mouth, he took her lips mouth in a hot, searing kiss that sent his heart on a rapid run. He kissed her with all that was in him, putting every promise and hope for the future into the kiss so that she knew to never, ever have any doubt that she was his one and only, now and forever.

They were concentrating on each other and the hot kiss that they didn't realize someone had joined them in the room.

"Mr. Bailey, I'm sorry, but visiting hours are over," the nurse attending to Loren said.

He broke the kiss off long enough to place the ring on her finger. He kissed her one last time then got up to leave, not wanting to give the nurse any problems by trying to overstay.

"Thank you nurse Kelly, I'm leaving now."

Mike turned back to Loren, gave her one last long, hot kiss before turning to leave.

"I love you baby. Get some sleep, don't give the staff any issues tonight and I promise to bring you more chocolate in the morning."

She smiled when he winked before finally leaving. Once he was gone, she snuggled deeper in the covers and marveled at the big, gorgeous ring he had just placed on her finger. She couldn't wait to show her family her new jewelry. She slid down in her bed, still looking at her ring and nodded off to sleep thinking of the life she would soon have with the man of her dreams.

Chapter 21

Mike arrived at the hospital to see Loren with two dozen white roses, a box of chocolates to ease Loren's craving for it and the biggest teddy bear he could find at the toy store for the baby. When he reached her room, he could tell she must have a lot of visitors because there was a lot of chatter. When he entered the room, all eyes turned to him and before he could even speak, Loren's mother came toward him and grabbed him tight.

"Loren's ring is beautiful Michael. I love it and I look forward to you finally, officially being a part of this family. Thank you for loving my daughter."

"Thank you for accepting me. You will never have to worry about Loren. I will always take very good care of her."

In the room along with Ms. Barbara, Mike also noticed Duron and Taija who were both congratulating Loren on the engagement. Duron then came toward him and they embraced in a brotherly hug. They would soon be brothers, well brothers-in-law, but brothers just the same.

"Welcome to the family Mike. I couldn't ask for a better brother."

"Thanks man. That means a lot coming from you."

As Duron stepped away, Taija also gave him a welcome to the family hug and kiss on the cheek.

"A wedding and a baby for you two. I'm very excited for you both," Taija said happily.

"Have you two set a date yet?" Ms. Barbara asked.

Loren responded first.

"No, we haven't set a date yet."

Mike then chimed in.

"I'd like the wedding to take place before the baby gets here. I want all parties involved to have my last name before my son or daughter gets here."

"As soon as I am able to walk, I am ready to walk down the aisle to become Mrs. Michael Bailey."

"It's going to be exciting helping you get everything together. I'm going to pick up some bridal magazines and bring them with me tomorrow so that you can get some ideas of what you want," her mother said.

"Whatever Loren wants is exactly what it will be," Mike said as he moved closer to Loren and gave her, her daily good morning kiss.

"In the meantime, Duron, we have to talk about the west coast office. With all of this, the accident, the baby and wedding and everything, I can't take responsibility for the west coast office. I need to be here with Loren and the baby. It was fine when it was just me, but I have a family to consider now and my life is here with them."

Loren was shocked to hear Mike pass on running the west coast branch of their company. She knew how much he was looking forward to moving and being closer to the family he had there. She couldn't let him give up the dream of doing that.

"Mike why would you give that up?"

He looked at her as he responded.

"I would give up everything for you. I know how close you are to your family and I know you love being close to them. I can stay here and continue to work in the Atlanta office here and Duron, Tyrone and I can work out what we'll do about the west coast office. It will work out baby, so don't worry."

"Wait. Do I have a say in this?" she asked. "Yes, I love my family very much, but my life is with you wherever that may be. I know you had your heart set on opening and running the west coast office and I want you to be able to do that."

"What about your company? You have your own business here in Atlanta as well," he said.

"I can run an interior design business from anywhere. Now that I'm also pregnant, I plan to limit the number of new projects I take on and I will let my assistants take over more of the day to day operations. I'm going to want to spend as much time as possible with the baby."

"Our life is wherever you want to make it and I say it's the west coast. We'll have the wedding here in Atlanta amongst all of our family and friends and then as soon as the baby is free to fly, we are moving to California where we will build our life. My parents can come out often to visit and so can the rest of the family. We can also visit them here in Atlanta whenever we want to. Don't give up your dream or even put it on hold. You can have it all and I'll be here to help you with whatever your dreams are."

Mike leaned down to kiss her to show her just how much more he loved her.

"I love you."

"I love you too," Loren said.

Duron interrupted the loving moment.

"Well now that you've cleared that up. Here is what we'll do. For now, Tyrone is going to fly out to the west coast to finalize everything so that you can be here with Loren as she recuperates. I knew you wouldn't want to leave her."

Everyone turned as Loren's dad came in the room. Duron continued sharing the business plans with everyone.

"Tyrone also still plans to attend the conference in Dallas, Texas in a few months that you were both going to. Don't worry about going with him. He said he can take care of it. For now, you only need to worry about taking care of my sister and making sure my niece or nephew is born healthy."

Mike was grateful for the great family he was about to become a part of by marriage.

Loren's dad, who had entered the room, asked if someone would bring him up to date on what everyone was talking about. Ms. Barbara spoke up.

"I'll fill you in when we get home later. For now, we are all going to just bask in the glow of the new baby, new son-in-law and a healthy daughter. I'm looking forward to two more grandchildren to add to the two I already have. I'll have to soon be baking more than one pack of cookies with all of these new babies coming."

Duron and Taija looked at each other curiously. When Taija nodded the okay to Duron, he interrupted his mother by telling everyone the added news about the baby they were having.

"Actually you will have three new grandchildren," Duron said.

"Three?" his mother asked.

"Yeah, mom. Taija is having twins. We just found out this week."

Ms. Barbara gave a squeal and gave Taija a tight hug. "I'm so happy for you."

"Thank you. We are very excited. We were a little scared at the news wondering what were we going to do with two babies at once, but that scare was quickly replaced with joy. We don't know the sex of the babies yet, but we both want to know."

"Okay everyone," Mr. Earl said. "Let's give Loren and Mike some breathing room."

Everyone gave Loren and Mike hugs and left the room, leaving them to bask in the news that not only were they having a baby and getting married, but that they were both looking forward to the move to the west coast to begin their life together.

"We're going to be very happy in California. I already know it," Loren said.

"Yes we are. Speaking of California, I need to talk to Tyrone about a few things before he heads that way. I also have a few things I need to go over with him about the Texas conference. I'm going to give him a call to see if he can meet up for dinner tonight to go over things."

Mike leaned down to give his wife the kind of kiss he really wanted to give her if the room had not been crowded. "I love you, the soon to be Mrs. Bailey.

Epilogue

Loren and Mike were taking a walk to continue to strengthen Loren's leg that had been broken. Now that the cast was off and Loren was up and about, it was important to continue exercising the leg to get it back to its regular strength. It had been a long recuperation, but here they were three months later and she was almost as good as new. The baby was growing well also. At four months, it was quite obvious that Loren was pregnant and she glowed. She was also happy that she and Mike had decided to get married before the baby was born. They decided against a very big wedding, but instead opted for a small gathering with close family and friends. In one more month, they would be husband and wife and Loren couldn't be happier.

They planned the wedding so that Loren would still be able to fly and make the move to California all before the baby was born instead of after. The west coast office was up and running and Mike needed to get back to work. He had flown out a few times over the past three months, making sure he wasn't gone too long from her. He was still worried about her recovery, but he still had a job to do. The successfulness of the new branch was dependent upon them moving forward. Loren was proud of Mike and she couldn't love him any more if she tried. He was her world. In the middle of them walking, Loren stopped suddenly, startling Mike.

"Loren, baby, what's wrong? Are you alright?"

Loren noticed the worried look on Mike's face.

"Yes I'm fine. Your son or daughter decided to give me a kick and it surprised me. This is the first time I have felt more than just a flutter in my stomach."

Mike reached down to caress her stomach and to speak to the baby.

"Alright now. No kicking mommy. Be nice in there and when you come out, I'll take you for some ice cream."

They laughed at his silliness.

Loren swatted his hand away and continued on with their walk. In the midst of preparing for the wedding, they were also waiting the birth of Duron and Taija's twin boys due in a few short months.

~~

Mike had just finished packing up the office in Loren's condo to have more of her things shipped to California when his phone rang. He looked at the screen and saw that it was Tyrone calling. Mike assumed Tyrone was calling about the conference he was attending to represent their business.

"Hey Ty. What's up man?"

"Not much. The conference is going well. I was asked to present tomorrow about modern structures. I'm looking forward to that. Say listen, a quick question. Do you remember the name of Taija's friend that came from

Boston to be in her wedding?"

Mike had to think for a minute.

"I don't know. Let me ask Loren."

Tyrone waited as Mike checked with Loren.

"Her name is Victoria Alston. Why what's up?"

"I think I saw her at the conference today. At least I think it was her or it was someone who looked just like her. I'll say hello later if I run into her again and see if it's her. If so, she looks good. I remember how fine she was when she was in town for the wedding. I may have tried to hook up with her if that girl I brought to the wedding didn't act like a second skin. I got rid of her right after that. I should have known better than to take a date to a wedding. What was I thinking?"

Mike laughed at his friend. He remembered those days. He happily gave them up for the current love of his life and wouldn't change a thing.

"Go for it man. Hope that works out for you. Don't forget Taija's baby shower is in two weeks and then my wedding next month. Don't bring any unwanted, clingy guests."

"Yeah, I hear you man. One day I'll learn. Until then, I'll hold down the single brother's club since you and Duron bailed on me. I guess it's just me against a world of beautiful, willing women and I certainly don't want to disappoint them. Give Loren a kiss for me and I'll see guys when I get back."

"Later man," Mike said, shaking his head at Tyrone. He knew that Tyrone wouldn't be singing that happy singles tune if he had found a woman like Loren. When he does, Mike dreaded the day Tyrone found the one. He couldn't imagine what all the single women of the world would do if

Tyrone was off the market too.

~~

Tyrone was about to head back into one of the breakout session rooms when he spotted the woman he thought was Taija's friend, Victoria. She was just as beautiful as he remembered her being at the wedding. Tyrone ventured in her direction to see if it was her and to say hello.

"Excuse me, but is your name Victoria Alston by any chance?"

"Yes it is," she replied.

"I thought that was you. My name is Tyrone. I'm best friends with Taija's husband Duron. I met you when you came to Atlanta to be in Taija's wedding."

Victoria could never forget him. She knew exactly who he was. She remembered him from the wedding and how sexy he looked in his all black tuxedo.

"I remember you, Tyrone. Nice to see you again. What are you doing here?"

"I'm speaking at the conference this week on modern design structure. What about you?"

"I work for a major financial corporation that deals with financing major construction projects and we are one of the vendors for the week."

Tyrone thought of how good his luck was.

"Since we are both here for this last night of the conference, would you join me for dinner later? We could dine right here at one of the restaurants in the hotel."

Victoria was not going to pass up the chance to sit across from this fine specimen of a man.

"I would love to."

She checked her watch and realized she needed to get to her last session of the day.

"I need to get into this last session. What time would you like for me to meet you?"

"Why don't we meet in the main lobby at eight o'clock? I'll make reservations at one of the restaurants, if that's okay with you."

"That's fine for me. I'll see you at eight Tyrone."

Victoria turned to head in the direction of her last session and smiled at the prospects of spending the evening with such a handsome man.

'Whew, what a man,' she silently said to herself.

~ ~

Tyrone watched Victoria walk away and couldn't help but notice her long, toned legs. He realized she had a magnificent pair. It just happens that his favorite part of a woman was her legs. Nicely toned, sculpted legs were a major turn on for him. He could imagine what hers would look like wrapped around his back as he entered her body over and over again while gripping on to her toned legs. He needed to clear his head and get to his own final session of the day. There would be time for elicit thoughts later on at dinner.

~ ~

Tyrone woke the next morning feeling great after a long night of sex with the most extraordinary woman he had ever met. After dinner he and Victoria could barely keep their hands off of each other as they made their way to his room. The rest of the night was a blur. He remembered enjoying the hottest sex of his life and he wanted more. He was glad he was waking up early. One more round of sex would be great. Besides, he loved early morning sex before starting his day.

He turned to reach for the very naked Victoria only to

discover the other side of the bed empty. He sat up and looked around for signs of her and realized she had left. He didn't see any of her clothes that were strewn around the room haphazardly from the night before when they couldn't wait to undress each other and get to the sheets. He got up to look around his suite, checking to see if she was in the bathroom. He looked, but no sign of her there. He went to the outer sitting area and again, no sign of Victoria. He was stunned that she would leave without even a goodbye after the night they had spent sexing each other every way possible known to man in the few hours they shared. He was hoping to see her again before she left. He had one more day at the conference, but he knew that she was leaving today because her last session was the day before. Tyrone decided to try and catch her before she left to find out why she dashed out on him. He called the receptionist desk to have them ring her room.

"Yes hello, this is Tyrone Davis. Can you ring room four twenty eight for me please, the room for Ms. Victoria Alston?"

"I'm sorry sir, but Ms. Alston has already checked out."

He wasn't happy with that information. It's quite obvious to him that Victoria wasn't happy about the events of the night before and was expecting to avoid it all together by leaving before he woke up. He smiled to himself. He knew for a fact that she couldn't avoid him forever. They would see each other again. A lot sooner than she thought. He knew for a fact that he would be seeing her at Taija's baby shower and he would ask her why she felt the need to leave like a thief in the night. The least she could have done was to leave the money on the night stand.

Tyrone moved about his room to prepare for his day knowing that he looked forward to seeing Victoria again and he had plans to make sure the one night they spent tasting each other would not be the one and only night.

'Be afraid Victoria. Be very afraid. I'm going to give you a little space, but not much. Now that I've had a taste, I want more of a meal,' Tyrone said to no one in particular.

Read more about Tyrone and Victoria in "A Perfect Combination" available now in paperback and for your e-pub device at www.cherylbarton.net.

Enjoy this excerpt from "Bachelor Not For Sale" the first in the bachelor series.

"I'm here to see Taija Charles," he said to the guard in the lobby of her office building as soon as he arrived.

"Sure sir. Take the elevators to your left to the eighth floor. The receptionist on that floor will show you to her office."

Duron thanked him and added a little more pep in his step as he made his way to the elevator that would take him to Taija.

When he reached the receptionist, who alerted Taija to his presence, he was escorted to her office where she sat behind her desk, finishing up a phone call. He liked that she smiled brightly when she saw him enter. When she completed her call, she got up and came around to greet him with the kind of kiss that he had come to enjoy. He also noticed that she was in her workout gear, not work attire.

"Is today dress down day at work or something?" he asked.

Taija looked down at herself, noticing she still had on gym clothes. She'd had a free morning and due to much stress at work, she'd decided to work out at the gym on the lower level of her office building. When she returned to her office, she'd spent time returning phone calls and had yet to go into the adjourning bathroom in her office to shower and change back into her work clothes.

"I went to work out this morning after a stressful meeting and haven't showered and changed yet. I was just about to when you arrived. So what brings you by today?"

Duron pulled her closer to him loving the feeling of

having her in his arms.

"I wanted to see you and to also see if you wanted to partake in an afternoon delight of lunch with me."

Taija loved how spontaneous Duron could be and she noticed a hint of a little something extra in the way he said lunch. Her body tingled thinking of the possibilities those words and the new smirk on his face could mean. Over the past several weeks that they had been seeing one another, she had experienced his spontaneity on more than a few occasions and the outcome had always been more than she could ever have imagined. She decided to play it cool and not be too eager to show him how much she wanted to do lunch with him and little something more. She gathered herself before responding.

"Of course. Lunch would be wonderful. Let me get out of these sweaty clothes, grab a shower and I'll be ready to go."

Duron watched the sway of Taija's hips as she made her way to her adjourning shower. His thoughts turned back to one morning a few weeks back when he entered his bedroom and Taija had been in the shower. He wanted to join her then, but she had just turned off the water and gotten out. The sight of her always turned him on and seeing her today was like seeing her for the first time. His body's response to her was instantaneous. He wasn't sure if Taija noticed how his body hardened the moment she came into his arms, but he knew of only one way to quench his body's thirst for her.

He heard her turn on the shower and wondered how adventurous he could get her to be. Without hesitating or second guessing his constant desire for her, he walked over to her office door, told her secretary that Taija asked if she could hold all of her calls. When her secretary smiled at him, knowing his intent, she acknowledged as he closed and locked the door. He wanted Taija bad and he wanted her now. He began taking off his own clothes as he headed for the bathroom shower to join her.

More books by this author can be found at
www.cherylbarton.

Now available for your reading pleasure:

Second Chances: Three Valentine Novellas
Sometimes love is better the second time around. Get
your copy and find out today!!

Down, But Not Out: Breaking Chains
Stories of three women who were down, but who should
never be counted out. You don't want to miss their
breakthrough when they discover what love from the right
man can do for them

Amorous Occupations Series
The Artist
The Bookkeeper
The Chef
The Dancer

About the Author

Cheryl Barton lives in Maryland where in her spare time she loves reading a few books a week, writing, spending time with her family, running her new publishing company, Barton Publishing, LLC and doing community service work through her non-profit organization, Sisters About Making Moves, which she founded in 2010. Her favorite downtime activity is eating Maryland steamed crabs. Visit her website at www.cherylbarton.net. You can connect with her on Twitter @mscbarton and on Facebook at Author Cheryl Barton.

Looking to publish your own novel? Contact Barton Publishing, LLC www.bartonpublishingLLC.com, where *Your Dreams Are Safe in Our Hands!*

Barton Book Publishing
P.O. Box 962
Reisterstown, Maryland 21136
443-379-3612
Email: Publisher@BartonpublishingLLC.com